HARBOR TALES DOWN NORTH

1871 1916

Norman Duncan

HARBOR TALES DOWN NORTH

BY

NORMAN DUNCAN

With an Appreciation by

WILFRED T. GRENFELL

ILLUSTRATED

Short Story Index Reprint Series

BOOKS FOR LIBRARIES PRESS
FREEPORT, NEW YORK

First Published 1918
Reprinted 1970

STANDARD BOOK NUMBER:
8369-3492-X

LIBRARY OF CONGRESS CATALOG CARD NUMBER:
72-121536

PRINTED IN THE UNITED STATES OF AMERICA

CONTENTS

ILLUSTRATIONS

NORMAN DUNCAN

An Appreciation by

WILFRED T. GRENFELL, M. D.

AS our thoughts fly back to the days when the writer of these stories was a guest aboard our little hospital vessel, we remember realizing how vast was the gulf which seemed to lie between him and the circumstances of our sea life in the Northland. Nowhere else in the world, perhaps, do the cold facts of life call for a more unrelieved material response. It is said of our people that they are born with a netting needle in their hand and an ax by the side of their cradle. Existence is a daily struggle with adamantine facts and conditions; and quick, practical response, which leaves little encouragement or opportunity for dreamers, is, often enough, the only dividing line between life and death. As I write these lines the greatest physical battle the world has ever seen is being fought. Yet here, as my eyes wander over the great ocean around me, nothing but absolute peace meets my view. But it too has its stormy times and its days when its strength and its mighty depths of possibilities are the most insistent points about it. And this spirit of the deep Norman Duncan seems to have understood as did no other of our visitors.

Our experience of the men from the hubs of existence had led us to regard them all as hardened by a keener struggle than ours, and critical, if not suspicious, of those who were satisfied to endure greater physical toil and discomfort than they for so much smaller material return. In the Labrador even a dog hates to be laughed at, and the merest suspicion of the supercilious makes a gap which it is almost impossible to bridge. But Norman Duncan created no such gap. He was, therefore, an anomaly to us—he was away below the surface—and few of us, during the few weeks he stayed, got to know him well enough to appreciate his real worth. Yet men who "go down to the sea in ships" have before now been known to sleep through a Grand Opera, or to see little to attract in the works of the Old Masters. And so we gather comfort for our inability to measure this man at his full stature.

All who love men of tender, responsive imagination loved Duncan. It was quite characteristic of the man that though he earned large sums of money by his pen, he was always so generous in helping those in need—more especially those who showed talents to which they were unable, through stress of circumstances, to give expression—that he died practically a poor man. He was a high-souled, generous idealist. All his work is purposeful, conveying to his readers a moral lesson. He had the keenest appreciation of the feelings of others and understood the immense significance of the little things of life—a fact evidenced by his vivid descriptions of the beauties of Nature, which he first appreciated and then, with his mastery of English, so ably described. His own experience of poverty and struggle after leaving the university opened to him channels for his sympathetic portrayal of humble life. Physically he was never a fighter or an athlete; but he proved himself possessed of singular personal courage. He fought his best fights, however, on fields to which gladiators have no entry and in battles which, unlike our physical contests, are not spasmodic, but increasing and eternal. Norman Duncan's love and affection for the people whom we also found joy in serving naturally endeared him to us. He was ever a true knight, entering the lists in behalf of those principles which make up man's real inner life; and we realize that his love for men who embody characteristics developed by constant contact with the sea—fortitude, simplicity, hardiness—died only with his own passing.

The stories here brought together are woven out of experiences gathered during his brief periods of contact with our life. But how real are his characters! Like other famous personalities in fiction —Mr. Pickwick, Ebenezer Scrooge, Colonel Newcome, Tom Jones, and a thousand others—who people a world we love, they teach us, possibly, more of high ideals, and of our capacities for service than do the actual lives of some saints, or the biographies of philosophers. And how vivid the action in which his characters take part! In the external circumstances of his life and in his literary art and preferences he was singularly like his elder brother in romance, Robert Louis Stevenson. Both were slight in physique but manly and vigorous in character and mission in life. Both were wanderers over the face of the globe. Both loved the sea passionately, and were at their best in telling of the adventures of those who spend their lives on the great waters. Both, finally, died at the height of power, literally with pen in hand, for both left recent and unfinished work. And the epitaph of either might well be the noble words of Stevenson from his brave essay on the greatness of the stout heart bound with triple brass:

"Death has not been suffered to take so much as an illusion from his heart. In the hot-fit of life, a-tiptoe on the highest point of being, he passes at a bound on the other side. The noise of the mallet and chisel is scarcely quenched, the trumpets are hardly done blowing, when, trailing clouds of glory, this happy-starred, full-blooded spirit shoots into the spiritual land."

BIOGRAPHICAL NOTE

IN the blood of Norman Duncan lived a spirit of romance and a love of adventure which make the chronicle of his short life a record of change and movement. He was born in Brantford, on the Grand River, in Western Ontario, July 2, 1871, and though he passed most of the years of his manhood in the United States, he never took out citizenship papers in the Republic. After a boyhood spent in various towns in Canada, he entered Toronto University, where in his four years of undergraduate life he participated eagerly in all forms of social and literary activity.

In 1895 he joined the reportorial staff of the *Auburn* (N. Y.) *Bulletin,* which position he held for two years. Then followed four years of congenial work on the staff of the *New York Evening Post,* where he served successively as reporter, copy editor on city desk, special writer for the city, and, finally, editor of the Saturday supplement. The editors of the *Post* were quick to recognize Duncan's ability in descriptive writing and character delineation, and under the spur of their encouragement he did his first important literary work, a series of short-stories of life in the Syrian quarter of New York City, published first in *The Atlantic Monthly* and *McClure's Magazine* and gathered subsequently into a book entitled *The Soul of the Street.* About the time of the appearance of this book the author's temperament reacted against the atmosphere which it embodied, and in the summer of 1900 by an arrangement with *McClure's Magazine* he went to Newfoundland to gather impressions and material for a series of sea-tales. Up to this time he had never spent a night on the ocean nor been at sea on a sailing vessel; in his boyhood he had rather feared the great gray ocean, and only later in life did he become so strongly attracted by its power and mystery and by the impression of its eternal struggle against those who must wrest a precarious living from its depths that it provided the background for his most striking and characteristic stories. Three summers in Newfoundland and one on the Labrador Coast resulted in *The Way of the Sea, Doctor Luke of the Labrador,* and other books and short-stories, including those of the present collection.

In 1901 Duncan was appointed assistant to the professor of English at Washington and Jefferson College, and one year later he was elected Wallace Professor of Rhetoric at the same institution, a post which he held until 1906. His duties were comparatively light so that he was able to devote much of his time to literary work. While occupying this position he enjoyed the companionship of his brother, Robert Kennedy Duncan, Professor of Chemistry at the college and later President of the Mellon Institute of the University of Pittsburgh, and the prominent author of a well-known series of text books in chemistry, who died in 1914.

In 1907 and 1908 Norman Duncan was special correspondent for *Harper's Magazine* in Palestine, Arabia, and Egypt, and in 1912 and 1913 he was sent by the same magazine to Australia, New Guinea, the Dutch East Indies, and the Malay States. Between these travel periods he acted for two years as adjunct professor of English at the University of Kansas. Not any of Duncan's foreign travel seems to have impressed him as did his visits to Newfoundland and the Labrador coast, and some of his best tales are those of the Northland—powerful stories of life reduced to its elements. Of these tales those of the present collection are a good representation.

The creator of these great stories was cut off at the height of his power; he died very suddenly of heart-disease while playing a golf-match in Fredonia, New York, on October 18, 1916. He lies buried in Brantford, Ontario, the town of his birth.

Few modern writers of tales and short-stories have drawn their materials from sources as scattered as those which attracted Norman Duncan. Among the immigrants of the East Side of New York, the rough lumber-jacks of the Northwest, and the trappers and deep-sea fishermen of Newfoundland and The Labrador he gathered his ideas and impressions. But though his characters and incidents are chosen from such diverse sources, the characteristics of his literary art remain constant in all his books, for the personality of the author did not change.

Norman Duncan was a realist in that he copied life. But his realism is that of Dickens and Bret Harte and Kipling rather than that of Mrs. Freeman and Arthur Morrison and the Russian story-tellers. He cared less for the accuracy of details than for the vividness of his general impressions and the force of his moral lessons. Like Bret Harte he idealized life. Like Harte, too, he was fond of dramatic situations and striking contrasts, of mixing the bitter and the sweet and the rough and the smooth of life; his introduction of the innocent baby into the drunkard-filled bar-room in *The Measure of a Man* is strikingly like Bret Harte's similar employment of this sentimental device in *The Luck of Roaring Camp,* and the presence of Patty Batch among the soiled women of Swamp's End in the same tale and of the tawdry Millie Slade face to face with the curate in *The Mother* is again reminiscent of Harte's technique. Like Dickens and like Bret Harte, Duncan was a frank moralist. His chief concern was in winnowing the souls of men and women bare of the chaff of petty circumstances which covered them. His stories all contain at least a minor chord of sentiment, but are usually free from the sentimentality which mars some of Harte's sketches. He is not ashamed to employ pathos, but his tragic situations are rarely overstrained and maudlin. He has all the tenderness of Dickens; his *Christmas Eve at Topmast Tickle* may well be compared with *A Christmas Carol.* Norman Duncan never married, but few Canadian or American authors have understood women as did the creator of high-spirited Bessie Roth and her noble mother in *Doctor Luke of the Labrador,* of naïve little Patty Batch, and of Millie Slade, glorified by her love for her son. In the delicacy and sensibility of his delineation of women he undoubtedly surpasses Bret Harte, most of whose women are either exaggerated or colorless. Moreover, Norman Duncan possessed a very genuine understanding of children, particularly of young boys, of whom he was exceedingly fond. There are few more sympathetic pictures of children in American literature than those of David Roth and the Lovejoy twins in *Doctor Luke of the Labrador,* and of Donald, Pale Peter's lad, in *The Measure of a Man;* and in Billy Topsail Duncan has created a real boy, a youngster as red-blooded and manly and keen for excitement in his numerous thrilling adventures in the frozen North as are any of Stevenson's boy heroes.

Variety and color in characters and situations, vividness of descriptions—especially in those of the stormy sea—rapidity of movement and dramatic intensity in narratives, genuine sentiment and real tenderness, humor, and pathos, and, above all, a healthy, vigorous, Anglo-Saxon morality—all of these qualities make of Norman Duncan's books and short-stories literature that is distinctly worthy and permanent in character.

I

MADMAN'S LUCK

I

MADMAN'S LUCK

IT was one thing or the other. Yet it might be neither. There was a disquieting alternative. No doubt the message disposed of the delicate affair for good and all in ten terse words. The maid had made up her mind; she had disclosed it in haste: that was all. It might be, however, that the dispatch conveyed news of a more urgent content. It might be that the maid lay ill—that she called for help and comfort. In that event, nothing could excuse the reluctance of the man who should decline an instant passage of Scalawag Run with the pitiful appeal. True, it was not inviting—a passage of Scalawag Run in the wet, gray wind, with night flowing in from the sea.

No matter about that. Elizabeth Luke had departed from Scalawag Harbor in confusion, leaving no definite answer to the two grave suggestions, but only a melting appeal for delay, as maids will—for a space of absence, an interval for reflection, an opportunity to search her heart and be sure of its decision. If, then, she had communicated that decision to her mother, according to her promise to communicate it to somebody, and if the telegram contained news of no more consequence, a good man might command his patience, might indulge in a reasonable caution, might hesitate on the brink of Black Cliff with the sanction of his self-respect. But if Elizabeth Luke lay ill and in need, a passage of Scalawag Run might be challenged, whatever came of it. And both Tommy Lark and Sandy Rowl knew it well enough.

Tommy Lark and Sandy Rowl, on the return from Bottom Harbor to Scalawag Run, had come to Point-o'-Bay Cove, where they were to lie the night. They were accosted in haste by the telegraph operator.

"Are you men from Scalawag?" she inquired.

She was a brisk, trim young woman from St. John's, new to the occupation, whose administration of the telegraph office was determined and exact.

"We is, ma'am," Sandy Rowl replied.

"It's fortunate I caught you," said the young woman, glowing with satisfaction. "Indeed it is! Are you crossing at once?"

Sandy Rowl smiled.

"We hadn't thought of it, ma'am," said he. "I 'low you don't know much about Scalawag Run," he added.

The young woman tossed her red head.

"When you *have* thought of it, and made up both your minds," she replied tartly, "you might let me know. It is a matter of some importance."

"Ay, ma'am."

By this time Tommy Lark had connected the telegraph operator's concern with the rare emergency of a message.

"What you so eager t' know for?" he inquired.

"I've a dispatch to send across."

"Not a telegram!"

"It is."

"Somebody in trouble?"

"As to that," the young woman replied, "I'm not permitted to say. It's a secret of the office."

"Is you permitted t' tell who the telegram is from?"

The young woman opened her eyes. This was astonishing simplicity. Permitted to tell who the telegram was from!

"I should think not!" she declared.

"Is you permitted t' tell who 'tis for?"

The young woman debated the propriety of disclosing the name. Presently she decided that no regulation of the office would be violated by a frank answer. Obviously she could not send the message without announcing its destination.

"Are you acquainted with Mrs. Jacob Luke?" said she.

Tommy Lark turned to Sandy Rowl. Sandy Rowl turned to Tommy Lark. Their eyes met. Both were concerned. It was Tommy Lark that replied.

"We is," said he. "Is the telegram for she?"

"It is."

"From Grace Harbor?"

"I'm not permitted to tell you that."

"Well then, if the telegram is for Mrs. Jacob Luke," said Tommy Lark gravely, "Sandy Rowl an' me will take a look at the ice in Scalawag Run an' see what we makes of it. I 'low we'll jus' *have* to. Eh, Sandy?"

Sandy Rowl's face was twisted with doubt. For a moment he deliberated. In the end he spoke positively.

"We'll take a look at it," said he.

They went then to the crest of Black Cliff to survey the ice in the run. Not a word was spoken on the way. A momentous situation, by the dramatic quality of which both young men were moved, had been precipitated by the untimely receipt of the telegram for Elizabeth Luke's mother.

Point-o'-Bay, in the lee of which the cottages of Point-o'-Bay Cove were gathered, as in the crook of a finger, thrust itself into the open sea. Scalawag Island, of which Scalawag Harbor was a sheltered cove, lay against the open sea. Between Point-o'-Bay and Scalawag Island was the run called Scalawag, of the width of two miles, leading from the wide open into Whale Bay, where it was broken and lost in the mist of the islands. There had been wind at sea—a far-off gale, perhaps, then exhausted, or plunging away into the southern seas, leaving a turmoil of water behind it.

Directly into the run, rolling from the open, the sea was swelling in gigantic billows. There would have been no crossing at all had there not been ice in the run; but there was ice in the run—plenty of ice, fragments of the fields in the Labrador drift, blown in by a breeze of the day before, and wallowing there, the wind having fallen away to a wet, gray breeze which served but to hold the ice in the bay.

It seemed, from the crest of Black Cliff, where Tommy Lark and Sandy Rowl stood gazing, each debating with his own courage, that the ice was heavy enough for the passage—thick ice, of varying extent, from fragments, like cracked ice, to wide pans; and the whole, it seemed, floated in contact, pan touching pan all the way across from the feet of Black Cliff to the first rocks of Scalawag Harbor.

What was inimical was the lift and fall of the ice in the great swells running in from the open sea.

"Well?" said Tommy Lark.

"I don't know. What do you think?"

"It might be done. I don't know."

"Ay; it might be. No tellin' for sure, though. The ice is in a wonderful tumble out there."

"Seems t' be heavy ice on the edge o' the sea."

"'Tis in a terrible commotion. I'd not chance it out there. I've never seed the ice so tossed about in the sea afore."

Tommy Lark reflected.

"Ay," he determined at last; "the best course across is by way o' the heavy ice on the edge o' the sea. There mus' be a wonderful steep slant t' some o' them pans when the big seas slips beneath them. Yet a man could go warily an' maybe keep from slidin' off. If the worst comes t' the worst, he could dig his toes an' nails in an' crawl. 'Tis not plain from here if them pans is touchin' each other all the way across; but it looks that way—I 'low they *is* touchin', with maybe a few small gaps that a man could get round somehow. Anyhow, 'tis not quite certain that a man would cast hisself away t' no purpose out there; an' if there's evil news in that telegram I 'low a man could find excuse enough t' try his luck."

"There's news both good and evil in it."

"I don't know," said Tommy Lark uneasily. "Maybe there is. 'Tis awful t' contemplate. I'm wonderful nervous, Sandy. Isn't you?"

"I is."

"Think the wind will rise? It threatens."

"I don't know. It has a sort of a switch to it that bodes a night o' temper. 'Tis veerin' t' the east. 'Twill be a gale from the open if it blows at all."

Tommy Lark turned from a listless contemplation of the gray reaches of the open sea.

"News both good an' evil!" he mused.

"The one for me an' the other for you. An' God knows the issue! I can't fathom it."

"I wish 'twas over with."

"Me too. I'm eager t' make an end o' the matter. 'Twill be a sad conclusion for me."

"I can't think it, Sandy. I thinks the sadness will be mine."

"You rouse my hope, Tommy."

"If 'tis not I, 'twill be you."

" 'Twill be you."

Tommy Lark shook his head dolefully. He sighed.

"Ah, no!" said he. "I'm not that deservin' an' fortunate."

"Anyhow, there's good news in that telegram for one of us," Sandy declared, "an' bad news for the other. An' whatever the news,—whether good for me an' bad for you, or good for you an' bad for me,—'tis of a sort that should keep for a safer time than this. If 'tis good news for you, you've no right t' risk a foot on the floe this night; if 'tis bad news for you, you might risk what you liked, an' no matter about it. 'Tis the same with me. Until we knows what's in that telegram, or until the fall of a better time than this for crossin' Scalawag Run, we've neither of us no right t' venture a yard from shore."

"You've the right of it, so far as you goes," Tommy Lark replied; "but the telegram may contain other news than the news you speaks of."

"No, Tommy."

"She said nothin' t' me about a telegram. She said she'd send a letter."

"She've telegraphed t' ease her mind."

"Why to her mother?"

"'Tis jus' a maid's way, t' do a thing like that."

"Think so, Sandy? It makes me wonderful nervous. Isn't you wonderful nervous, Sandy?"

"I am that."

"I'm wonderful curious, too. Isn't you?"

"I is. I'm impatient as well. Isn't you?"

"I'm havin' a tough struggle t' command my patience. What you think she telegraphed for?"

"Havin' made up her mind, she jus' couldn't wait t' speak it."

"I wonder what——"

"Me too, Sandy. God knows it! Still an' all, impatient as I is, I can wait for the answer. 'Twould be sin an' folly for a man t' take his life out on Scalawag Run this night for no better reason than t' satisfy his curiosity. I'm in favor o' waitin' with patience for a better time across."

"The maid might be ill," Tommy Lark objected.

"She's not ill. She's jus' positive an' restless. I knows her ways well enough t' know that much."

"She *might* be ill."

"True, she might; but she——"

"An' if——"

Sandy Rowl, who had been staring absently up the coast toward the sea, started and exclaimed.

"Ecod!" said he. "A bank o' fog's comin' round Point-o'-Bay!"

"Man!"

"That ends it."

"'Tis a pity!"

"'Twill be thick as mud on the floe in half an hour. We must lie the night here."

"I don't know, Sandy."

Sandy laughed.

"Tommy," said he, "'tis a wicked folly t' cling t' your notion any longer."

"I wants t' know what's in that telegram."

"So does I."

"I'm fair shiverin' with eagerness t' know. Isn't you?"

"I'm none too steady."

"Sandy, I jus' *got* t' know!"

"Well, then," Sandy Rowl proposed, "we'll go an' bait the telegraph lady into tellin' us."

It was an empty pursuit. The young woman from St. John's was obdurate. Not a hint escaped her in response to the baiting and awkward interrogation of Tommy Lark and Sandy Rowl; and the more they besought her, the more suspicious she grew. She was an obstinate young person—she was precise, she was scrupulous, she was of a secretive, untrustful turn of mind; and as she was ambitious for advancement from the dreary isolation of Point-o'-Bay Cove, she was not to be entrapped or entreated into what she had determined was a breach of discipline. Moreover, it appeared to her suspicious intelligence that these young men were too eager for information. Who were they? She had not been long in charge of the office at Point-o'-Bay Cove. She did not know them. And why should they demand to know the contents of the telegram before undertaking the responsibility of its delivery?

As for the degree of peril in a crossing of Scalawag Run, she was not aware of it; she was from St. John's, not out-port born. The ice in the swell of the sea, with fog creeping around Point-o'-Bay in a rising wind, meant nothing to her experience. At any rate, she would not permit herself to fall into a questionable situation in which she might be called severely to account. She was not of that sort. She had her own interests to serve. They would be best served by an exact execution of her duty.

"This telegram," said she, "is an office secret, as I have told you already. I have my orders not to betray office secrets."

Tommy Lark was abashed.

"Look you," he argued. "If the message is of no consequence an' could be delayed——"

"I haven't said that it is of no consequence."

"Then *'tis* of consequence!"

"I don't say that it is of consequence. I don't

say anything either way. I don't say anything at all."

"Well, now," Tommy complained, "t' carry that message across Scalawag Run would be a wonderful dangerous——"

"You don't have to carry it across."

"True. Yet 'tis a man's part t' serve——"

"My instructions," the young woman interrupted, "are to deliver messages as promptly as possible. If you are crossing to Scalawag Harbor to-night, I should be glad if you would take this telegram with you. If you are not—well, that's not my affair. I am not instructed to urge anybody to deliver my messages."

"Is the message from the maid?"

"What a question!" the young woman exclaimed indignantly. "I'll not tell you!"

"Is there anything about sickness in it?"

"I'll not tell you."

"If 'tis a case o' sickness," Tommy declared, "we'll take it across, an' glad t' be o' service. If 'tis the other matter——"

"What other matter?" the young woman flashed.

"Well," Tommy replied, flushed and awkward, "there was another little matter between Elizabeth Luke an'——"

The young woman started.

"Elizabeth Luke!" she cried. "Did you say Elizabeth Luke?"

"I did, ma'am."

"I said nothing about Elizabeth Luke."

"We knows 'tis from she."

"Ah-ha!" the young woman exclaimed. "You know far too much. I think you have more interest in this telegram than you ought to have."

"I confess it."

The young woman surveyed Tommy Lark with sparkling curiosity. Her eyes twinkled. She pursed her lips.

"What's your name?" she inquired.

"Thomas Lark."

The young woman turned to Sandy Rowl.

"What's your name?" she demanded.

"Alexander Rowl. Is there—is there anything in the telegram about me? Aw, come now!"

The young woman laughed pleasantly. There was a romance in the wind. Her interest was coy.

"Would you like to know?" she teased, her face dimpling.

Sandy Rowl responded readily to this dimpling, flashing banter. A conclusion suggested itself with thrilling conviction.

"I would!" he declared.

"And to think that I could tell you!"

"I'm sure you could, ma'am!"

The young woman turned to Tommy Lark.

"Your name's Lark?"

"Yes, ma'am. There's nothin'—there's nothin' in the telegram about a man called Thomas Lark, is there?"

"And yours is Rowl?"

"Yes, ma'am."

"I'm new to these parts," said the young woman, "and I'm trying to learn all the names I can master. Now, as for this telegram, you may take it or leave it, just as you will. What are you going to do? I want to close the office now and go home to tea."

"We'll take it," said Sandy Rowl. "Eh, Tommy?"

"Ay."

"An' we'll deliver it as soon as we're able. It may be the night. It may not be. What say t' that, Tommy?"

"We'll take it across."

With that the young woman handed the sealed envelope to Tommy Lark and bade them both good-night.

Tommy Lark thrust the telegram in his waistcoat pocket and buttoned his jacket. Both men turned to the path to the crest of Black Cliff, whence a lesser foot-path led to the shore of the sea.

"One o' the two of us," said Sandy Rowl, "is named in that telegram. I'm sure of it."

Tommy Lark nodded.

"I knows it," Sandy proceeded, "because I seed a flicker in the woman's eye when she learned the two names of us. She's a sly one, that young woman!"

"Ay."

"You is chosen, Tommy."

"No, 'tis not I. 'Tis you. You is selected, Sandy. The woman twinkled when she named you. I marked it t' my sorrow."

"The maid would not choose me, Tommy," Sandy replied, his face awry with a triumphant smile, "when she might have you."

"She've done it."

In advance, on the path to the crest of Black Cliff, Tommy Lark was downcast and grim. Of a faithful, kindly nature in respect to his dealings with others, and hopeful for them all, and quick with an inspiring praise and encouragement, he could discover no virtue in himself, nor had he any compassion when he phrased the chapters of his own future; and though he was vigorous and decisive in action, not deterred by the gloom of any prospect, he was of a gray, hopeless mind in a crisis.

Rowl, however, was of a saucy, sanguine temperament; his faith in his own deserving was never diminished by discouragement; nor, whatever his lips might say, was he inclined to foresee in his future any unhappy turn of fortune. The telegraph operator, he was persuaded, had disclosed an understanding of the situation in a twinkle of her blue eyes and an amused twist of her thin lips; and the twinkle and the twist had indicated the presence of his name in Elizabeth Luke's telegram. Rowl was uplifted—triumphant.

In the wake of Tommy Lark he grinned, his teeth bare with delight and triumph. And as for Tommy Lark, he plodded on, striving grimly up the hill, his mind sure of its gloomy inference, his heart wrenched, his purpose resolved upon a worthy course of feeling and conduct. Let the dear maid have her way! She had chosen her happiness. And with that a good man must be content.

In the courtship of pretty Elizabeth Luke, Tommy Lark had acted directly, bluntly, impetuously, according to his nature. And he had been forehanded with his declaration. It was known to him that Sandy Rowl was pressing the same pursuit to a swift conclusion. Tommy Lark loved the maid. He had told her so with indiscreet precipitation; and into her confusion he had flung the momentous question.

"Maid," said he, "I loves you! Will you wed me?"

Sandy Rowl, being of a more subtle way in all things, had proceeded to the issue with delicate caution, creeping toward it by inches, as a man stalks a caribou. He too had been aware of rivalry; and, having surmised Tommy Lark's intention, he had sought the maid out unwittingly, not an hour after her passionate adventure with Tommy Lark, and had then cast the die of his own happiness.

In both cases the effect had been the same. Elizabeth Luke had wept and fled to her mother like a frightened child; and she had thereafter protested, with tears of indecision, torn this way and that until her heart ached beyond endurance, that she was not sure of her love for either, but felt that she loved both, nor could tell whom she loved the most, if either at all. In this agony of confusion, terrifying for a maid, she had fled beyond her mother's arms, to her grandmother's cottage at Grace Harbor, there to deliberate and decide, as she said; and she had promised to speed her conclusion with all the determination she could command, and to return a letter of decision.

In simple communities, such as Scalawag Harbor, a telegram is a shocking incident. Bad news must be sped; good news may await a convenient time. A telegram signifies the very desperation of haste and need—it conveys news only of the most momentous import; and upon every man into whose hands it falls it lays a grave obligation to expedite its delivery. Tommy Lark had never before touched a telegram; he had never before clapped eyes on one. He was vaguely aware of the telegram as a mystery of wire and a peculiar cunning of men. Telegrams had come to Scalawag Harbor in times of disaster in the course of Tommy Lark's nineteen years of life. Widow Mull, for example, when the *White Wolf* was cast away at the ice, with George Mull found frozen on the floe, had been told of it in a telegram.

All the while, thus, Tommy Lark's conception of

the urgency of the matter mounted high and oppressed him. Elizabeth Luke would not lightly dispatch a telegram from Grace Harbor to her mother at Scalawag. All the way from Grace Harbor? Not so! After all, this could be no message having to do with the affairs of Tommy Lark and Sandy Rowl. Elizabeth would not have telegraphed such sentimental news. She would have written a letter. Something was gone awry with the maid. She was in trouble. She was in need. She was ill. She might be dying. And the more Tommy Lark reflected, as he climbed the dripping Black Cliff path, the more surely was his anxious conviction of Elizabeth Luke's need confirmed by his imagination.

When Tommy Lark and Sandy Rowl came to the crest of Black Cliff, a drizzle of rain was falling in advance of the fog. The wind was clipping past in soggy gusts that rose at intervals to the screaming pitch of a squall. A drab mist had crept around Point-o'-Bay and was spreading over the ice in Scalawag Run. Presently it would lie thick between Scalawag Island and the mainland of Point-o'-Bay Cove.

At the edge of the ice, where the free black water of the open met the huddled floe, the sea was breaking. There was a tossing line of white water—the crests of the breakers flying away in spindrift like long white manes in the wind. Even from the crest of Black Cliff, lifted high above the ice and water of the gray prospect below, it was plain that a stupendous sea was running in from the darkening open, slipping under the floe, swelling through the run, and subsiding in the farthest reaches of the bay.

From the broken rock of Black Cliff to the coast of Scalawag Run, two miles beyond, where Scalawag Harbor threatened to fade and vanish in the fog and falling dusk, the ice was in motion, great pans of the pack tossing like chips in the gigantic waves. Nowhere was the ice at rest. It was neither heavy enough nor yet sufficiently close packed to flatten the sea with its weight. And a survey of the creeping fog and the ominous approach of a windy night portended that no more than an hour of drab light was left for the passage.

" 'Tis a perilous task t' try," said Tommy Lark. "I never faced such a task afore. I fears for my life."

" 'Tis a madcap thing t' try!"

"Ay, a madcap thing. A man will need madman's luck t' come through with his life."

"Pans as steep as a roof out there!"

"Slippery as butter, Sandy. 'Twill be ticklish labor t' cling t' some o' them when the sea cants them high. I wish we had learned t' swim, Sandy, when we was idle lads t'gether. We'll sink like two jiggers if we slips into the water. Is you comin' along, Sandy? It takes but one man t' bear a message. I'll not need you."

"Tommy," Sandy besought, "will you not listen t' reason an' wisdom?"

"What wisdom, Sandy?"

"Lave us tear open the telegram an' read it."

"Hoosh!" Tommy ejaculated. "Such a naughty trick as that! I'll not do it. I jus' couldn't."

" 'Tis a naughty trick that will save us a pother o' trouble."

"I'm not chary o' trouble in the maid's behalf."

" 'Twill save us peril."

"I've no great objection t' peril in her service. I'll not open the telegram; I'll not intrude on the poor maid's secrets. Is you comin' along?"

Sandy Rowl put a hand on Tommy Lark's shoulder.

"What moves you," said he impatiently, "to a mad venture like this, with the day as far sped as it is?"

"I'm impelled."

"What drives you?"

"The maid's sick."

"Huh!" Sandy scoffed. "A lusty maid like that! She's not sick. As for me, I'm easy about her health. She's as hearty at this minute as ever she was in her life. An' if she isn't, we've no means o' bein' sure that she isn't. 'Tis mere guess-work. We've no certainty of her need. T' be drove out on the ice o' Scalawag Run by the guess-work o' fear an' fancy is a folly. 'Tis not demanded.

We've every excuse for lyin' the night at Point-o'-Bay Cove."

"I'm not seekin' excuse."

"You've no need to seek it. It thrusts itself upon you."

"Maybe. Yet I'll have none of it. 'Tis a craven thing t' deal with."

"'Tis mere caution."

"Well, well! I'll have no barter with caution in a case like this. I crave service. Is you comin' along?"

Sandy Rowl laughed his disbelief.

"Service!" said he. "You heed the clamor o' your curiosity. That's all that stirs you."

"No," Tommy Lark replied. "My curiosity asks me no questions now. Comin' up the hill, with this here telegram in my pocket, I made up my mind. 'Tis not I that the maid loves. It couldn't be. I'm not worthy. Still an' all, I'll carry her message t' Scalawag Harbor. An' if I'm overcome I'll not care very much—save that 'twill sadden me t' know at the last that I've failed in her service. I've no need o' you, Sandy. You've no call to come. You may do what you likes an' be no less a man. As you will, then. Is you comin'?"

Sandy reflected.

"Tommy," said he then, reluctantly, "will you listen t' what I should tell you?"

"I'll listen."

"An' will you believe me an' heed me?"

"I'll believe you, Sandy."

"You've fathomed the truth o' this matter. 'Tis not you that the maid loves. 'Tis I. She've not told me. She've said not a word that you're not aware of. Yet I knows that she'll choose me. I've loved more maids than one. I'm acquainted with their ways. An' more maids than one have loved me. I've mastered the signs o' love. I've studied them; I reads them like print. It pleases me t' see them an' read them. At first, Tommy, a maid will not tell. She'll not tell even herself. An' then she's overcome; an', try as she may to conceal what she feels, she's not able at all t' do it. The signs, Tommy? Why, they're all as plain in speech as words themselves could be! Have you seed any signs, boy? No. She'll not wed you. 'Tis not in her heart t' do it, whatever her mind may say. She'll wed me. I knows it. An' so I'll tell you that you'll waste your labor if you puts out on Scalawag Run with the notion o' winnin' the love o' this maid with bold behavior in her service. If that's in your mind, put it away. Turn with me t' Point-o'-Bay Cove an' lie safe the night. I'm sorry, Tommy. You'll grieve, I knows, t' lose the maid. I could live without her. True. There's other maids as fair as she t' be found in the world. Yet I loves this maid more than any maid that ever I knowed; an' I'd be no man at all if I yielded her to you because I pitied your grief."

"I'm not askin' you t' yield her."

"Nor am I wrestin' her away. She've jus' chose for herself. Is she ever said she cared for you, Tommy?"

"No."

"Is there been any sign of it?"

"She've not misled me. She've said not a word that I could blame her for. She—she've been timid in my company. I've frightened her."

"She's merry with me."

"Ay."

"Her tongue jus' sounds like brisk music, an' her laughter's as free as a spring o' water."

"She've showed me no favor."

"Does she blush in your presence?"

"She trembles an' goes pale."

"Do her eyes twinkle with pleasure?"

"She casts them down."

"Does she take your arm an' snuggle close?"

"She shrinks from me."

"Does she tease you with pretty tricks?"

"She does not," poor Tommy replied. "She says, 'Yes, sir!' an' 'No, sir!' t' me."

"Ha!" Sandy exclaimed. "'Tis I that she'll wed!"

"I'm sure of it. I'm content t' have her follow her will in all things. I loves the maid. I'll not pester her with complaint. Is you comin' along?"

"'Tis sheer madness!"

"Is you comin' along?"

Sandy Rowl swept his hand over the prospect of fog and spindrift and wind-swept ice.

"Man," he cried, "look at that!"

"The maid's sick," Tommy Lark replied doggedly. "I loves her. Is you comin' along?"

"You dunderhead!" Sandy Rowl stormed. "I got t' go! Can't you understand that? You leaves me no choice!"

When Tommy Lark and Sandy Rowl had leaped and crept through half the tossing distance to Scalawag Harbor, the fog had closed in, accompanied by the first shadows of dusk, and the coast and hills of Scalawag Island were a vague black hulk beyond, slowly merging with the color of the advancing night. The wind was up—blowing past with spindrift and a thin rain; but the wind had not yet packed the ice, which still floated in a loose, shifting floe, spotted and streaked with black lakes and lanes of open water. They had taken to the seaward edge of the pack for the advantage of heavier ice.

A line of pans, sluggish with weight, had lagged behind in the driving wind of the day before, and was now closing in upon the lighter fragments of the pack, which had fled in advance and crowded the bay. Whatever advantage the heavier ice offered in the solidity of its footing, and whatever in the speed with which it might be traversed by agile, daring men, was mitigated by another condition involved in its exposed situation. It lay against the open sea; and the sea was high, rolling directly into Scalawag Run, in black, lofty billows, crested with seething white in the free reaches of the open. The swells diminished as they ran the length of the run and spent themselves in the bay. Their maximum of power was at the edge of the ice.

In Scalawag Run, thus, the ice was like a strip of shaken carpet—its length rolling in lessening waves from first to last, as when a man takes the corners of an end of the strip and snaps the whole to shake the dust out of it; and the spindrift, blown in from the sea and snatched from the lakes in the mist of the floe, may be likened to clouds of white dust, half realized in the dusk.

As the big seas slipped under the pack, the pans rose and fell; they were never at rest, never horizontal, except momentarily, perhaps, on the crest of a wave and in the lowest depths of a trough. They tipped—pitched and rolled like the deck of a schooner in a gale of wind. And as the height of the waves at the edge of the ice may fairly be estimated at thirty feet, the incline of the pans was steep and the surface slippery.

Much of the ice lying out from Point-o'-Bay was wide and heavy. It could be crossed without peril by a sure-footed man. Midway of the run, however, the pans began to diminish in size and to thin in quantity; and beyond, approaching the Scalawag coast, where the wind was interrupted by the Scalawag hills, the floe was loose and composed of a field of lesser fragments. There was still a general contact—pan lightly touching pan; but many of the pans were of an extent so precariously narrow that their pitching surface could be crossed only on hands and knees, and in imminent peril of being flung off into the gaps of open water.

It was a feat of lusty agility, of delicate, experienced skill, of steadfast courage, to cross the stretches of loose ice, heaving, as they were, in the swell of the sea. The foothold was sometimes impermanent—blocks of ice capable of sustaining the weight of a man through merely a momentary opportunity to leap again; and to the scanty chance was added the peril of the angle of the ice and the uncertainty of the path beyond.

Once Tommy Lark slipped when he landed on an inclined pan midway of a patch of water between two greater pans. His feet shot out and he began to slide feet foremost into the sea, with increasing momentum, as a man might fall from a steep, slimy roof. The pan righted in the trough, however, to check his descent over the edge of the ice. When it reached the horizontal in the depths of the trough, and there paused before responding to the lift of the next wave, Tommy Lark caught his feet; and he was set and balanced against the tip and fling of the pan in the other direction as the wave slipped beneath and ran on. When the ice was flat and stable on the crest of the sea, he leaped from the heavy pan beyond, and then threw himself down to rest and recover from the shudder and daze of the fate he had escaped. And the dusk was falling all the while, and the fog, closing in, thickened the dusk, threatening to turn it impenetrable to the beckoning lights in the cottages of Scalawag Harbor.

Having come, at last, to a doubtful lane, sparsely spread with ice, Tommy Lark and Sandy Rowl were halted. They were then not more than half a mile from the rocks of Scalawag. From the substantial ground of a commodious block, with feet spread to brace themselves against the pitch of the pan as a man stands on a heaving deck, they appraised the chances and were disheartened. The lane was like a narrow arm of the sea, extending, as nearly as could be determined in the dusk, far into the floe; and there was an opposite shore—another commodious pan. In the black water of the arm there floated white blocks of ice. Some were manifestly substantial: a leaping man could pause to rest; but many—necessary pans, these, to a crossing of the lane—were as manifestly incapable of bearing a man up.

As the pan upon which Tommy Lark and Sandy Rowl stood lay near the edge of the floe, the sea was running up the lane in almost undiminished swells—the long, slow waves of a great ground swell, not a choppy wind-lop, but agitated by the wind and occasionally breaking. It was a thirty-foot sea in the open. In the lane it was somewhat less—not much, however; and the ice in the lane and all round about was heaving in it—tumbled about, rising and falling, the surface all the while at a changing slant from the perpendicular.

Rowl was uneasy.

"What you think, Tommy?" said he. "I don't like t' try it. I 'low we better not."

"We can't turn back."

"No; not very well."

"There's a big pan out there in the middle. If a man could reach that he could choose the path beyond."

" 'Tis not a big pan."

"Oh, 'tis a fairish sort o' pan."

" 'Tis not big enough, Tommy."

Tommy Lark, staggering in the motion of the ice, almost off his balance, peered at the pan in the middle of the lane."

" 'Twould easily bear a man," said he.

" 'Twould never bear two men."

"Maybe not."

"Isn't no 'maybe' about it," Rowl declared. "I'm sure 'twouldn't bear two men."

"No," Tommy Lark agreed. "I 'low 'twouldn't."

"A man would cast hisself away tryin' t' cross on that small ice."

"I 'low he might."

"Well, then," Rowl demanded, "what we goin' t' do?"

"We're goin' t' cross, isn't we?"

" 'Tis too parlous a footin' on them small cakes."

"Ay; 'twould be ticklish enough if the sea lay flat an' still all the way. An' as 'tis——"

" 'Tis like leapin' along the side of a steep."

"Wonderful steep on the side o' the seas."

"Too slippery, Tommy. It can't be done. If a man didn't land jus' right he'd shoot off."

"That he would, Sandy!"

"Well?"

"I'll go first, Sandy. I'll start when we lies in the trough. I 'low I can make that big pan in the middle afore the next sea cants it. You watch me, Sandy, an' practice my tactics when you follow. I 'low a clever man can cross that lane alive."

"We're in a mess out here!" Sandy Rowl complained. "I wish we hadn't started."

" 'Tisn't so bad as all that."

"A loud folly!" Rowl growled.

"Ah, well," Tommy Lark replied, "a telegram's a telegram; an' the need o' haste——"

" 'Twould have kept well enough."

" 'Tis not a letter, Sandy."

"Whatever it is, there's no call for two men t' come into peril o' their lives——"

"You never can tell."

"I'd not chance it again for——"

"We isn't drowned yet."

"Yet!" Rowl exclaimed. "No—not yet! We've a minute or so for prayers!"

Tommy Lark laughed.

"I'll get under way now," said he. "I'm not so very much afraid o' failin'."

There was no melodrama in the situation. It was a commonplace peril of the coast; it was a reasonable endeavor. It was thrilling, to be sure—the conjunction of a living peril with the emergency of the message. Yet the dusk and sweeping drizzle of rain, the vanishing lights of Scalawag Harbor, the interruption of the lane of water, the mounting seas, their declivities flecked with a path of treacherous ice, all were familiar realities to Tommy Lark and Sandy Rowl. Moreover, a telegram was not a letter. It was an urgent message. It imposed upon a man's conscience the obligation to speed it. It should be delivered with determined expedition. Elsewhere, in a rural community, for example, a good neighbor would not hesitate to harness his horse on a similar errand and travel a deep road of a dark night in the fall of the year; nor, with the snow falling thick, would he confront a midnight trudge to his neighbor's house with any louder complaint than a fretful growl.

It was in this spirit, after all, touched with an intimate solicitude which his love for Elizabeth Luke aroused, that Tommy Lark had undertaken the passage of Scalawag Run. The maid was ill—

her message snould be sped. As he paused on the brink of the lane, however, waiting for the ice to lie flat in the trough, poised for the spring to the first pan, a curious apprehension for the safety of Sandy Rowl took hold of him, and he delayed his start.

"Sandy," said he, "you be careful o' yourself."

"I will that!" Sandy declared. He grinned. "You've no need t' warn me, Tommy," he added.

"If aught should go amiss with you," Tommy explained, " 'twould be wonderful hard—on Elizabeth."

Sandy Rowl caught the honest truth and unselfishness of the warning in Tommy Lark's voice.

"I thanks you, Tommy," said he. " 'Twas well spoken."

"Oh, you owes me no thanks," Tommy replied simply. "I'd not have the maid grieved for all the world."

"I'll tell her that you said so."

Tommy was startled.

"You speak, Sandy," said he in gloomy foreboding, "as though I had come near t' my death."

"We've both come near t' death."

"Ay—maybe. Well—no matter."

" 'Tis a despairful thing to say."

"I'm not carin' very much what happens t' my life," young Tommy declared. "You'll mind that said so. An' I'm glad that I isn't carin' very much any more. Mark that, Sandy—an' re-member."

Between the edge of Tommy Lark's commodious pan and the promising block in the middle of the lane lay five cakes of ice. They varied in size and weight; and they were swinging in the swell—climbing the steep sides of the big waves, riding the crests, slipping downhill, tipped to an angle, and lying flat in the trough of the seas. In respect to their distribution they were like stones in a brook: it was a zigzag course—the intervals varied. Leaping from stone to stone to cross a brook, using his arms to maintain a balance, a man can not pause; and his difficulty increases as he leaps—he grows more and more confused, and finds it all the while harder to keep upright. What he fears is a mossy stone and a rolling stone. The small cakes of ice were as slippery as a mossy stone in a brook, and as treacherously unstable as a rolling stone; and in two particulars they were vastly more difficult to deal with; they were all in motion, and not one of them would bear the weight of a man. There was more ice in the lane. It was a mere scattering of fragments and a gathered patch or two of slush.

Tommy Lark's path to the pan in the middle of the lane was definite: the five small cakes of ice—he must cover the distance in six leaps without pause; and, having come to the middle of the lane, he could rest and catch his breath while he chose out the course beyond. If there chanced to be no path beyond, discretion would compel an immediate return.

"Well," said he, crouching for the first leap, "I'm off, whatever comes of it!"

"Mind the slant o' the ice!"

"I'll take it in the trough."

"Not yet!"

Tommy Lark waited for the sea to roll on.

"You bother me," he complained. "I might have been half way across by this time."

"You'd have been cotched on the side of a swell. If you're cotched like that you'll slip off the ice. There isn't a man livin' can cross that ice on the slant of a sea."

"Be still!"

The pan was subsiding from the incline of a sea to the level of the trough.

"Now!" Sandy Rowl snapped.

When the ice floated in the trough, Tommy Lark leaped, designing to attain his objective as nearly as possible before the following wave lifted his path to an incline. He landed fairly in the middle of the first cake, and had left it for the second before it sank. The second leap was short. It was difficult, nevertheless, for two reasons. He had no time to gather himself for the impulse, and his flight was taken from sinking ground. Almost he fell short. Six inches less, and he would have landed on the edge of the cake and toppled back into the sea

"Well, I'm off, whatever comes of it."

when it tipped to the sudden weight. But he struck near enough to the center to restrain the ice, in a few active steps, from sinking by the edge; and as the second cake was more substantial than the first, he was able to leap with confidence for the third, whence he danced lightly toward the fourth.

The fourth cake, however, lay abruptly to the right. A sudden violent turn was required to reach it. It was comparatively substantial; but it was rugged rather than flat—there was a niggardly, treacherous surface for landing, and as ground for a flight the cake furnished a doubtful opportunity. There was no time for recovery. When Tommy Lark landed, the ice began to waver and sink. He had landed awkwardly, his feet in a tangle; and, as there was no time for placing his feet in a better way, he must leap awkwardly—leap instantly, leaving the event to chance. And leap he did. It was a supreme effort toward the fifth cake.

By this time the ice was fast climbing the side of a swelling wave. The crest of the sea was higher than Tommy Lark's head. Had the sea broken it would have fallen on him—it would have submerged and overwhelmed him. It did not break. The wind snatched a thin spindrift from the crest and flung it past like a squall of rain. That was all. Tommy Lark was midway of the sea, as a man might be on the side of a steep hill: there was the crest above and the trough below; and the fifth cake of ice was tipped to an increasingly perilous angle. Moreover, it was small; it was the least of all—a momentary foothold, to be touched lightly in passing on to the slant of the wide pan in the middle of the lane.

All this was clear to Tommy Lark when he took his awkward leap from the fourth cake. What he feared was less the meager proportions of the fifth cake—which would be sufficient, he fancied, to give him an impulse for the last leap—than the slant of the big pan to which he was bound, which was precisely as steep as the wave it was climbing. And this fear was justified by the event. Tommy Lark touched the little cake with the toe of his sealhide boot, with the sea then nearing its climax, and alighted prostrate on the smooth slant of the big pan. He grasped for handhold: there was none; and, had not the surface of the pan been approaching a horizontal on the crest of the sea, he would have shot over the edge. Nothing else saved him.

Tommy Lark rose and established his balance with widespread feet and waving arms.

" 'Tis not too bad," he called.

"What's beyond?"

"No trouble beyond."

There was more ice beyond. It was small. Tommy Lark danced across to the other side of the lane, however, without great difficulty. He could not have paused on the way. The ice, thick though it was, was too light.

"Safe over!" he shouted.

"I'm comin'."

"Mind the leap for the big pan. 'Tis a ticklish landin'. That's all you've t' fear."

Sandy Rowl was as agile as Tommy Lark. He was as competent—he was as practiced. Following the same course as Tommy Lark, he encountered the same difficulties and met them in the same way; and thus he proceeded from the first sinking cake through the short leap to the second more substantial one, whence he leaped with confidence to the third, landed on the rugged fourth, his feet ill placed for the next leap, and sprang awkwardly for the small fifth cake, meaning to touch it lightly on his course to the big pan.

But he had started an instant too soon. When, therefore, he came to the last leap, with the crest of the wave above him and the trough below, the pan was midway of the side of the sea, its inclination at the widest. He slipped—fell; and he rolled off into the water and sank. When he came to the surface, the ice was on the crest of the sea, beginning its descent. He grasped the edge of it and tried to draw himself aboard. In this he failed. The pan was too thick—too high in the water; and the weight of his boots and clothes was too great to overcome. In the trough of the sea, where his opportunity was best, he almost succeeded. He established one knee on the pan and strove desperately and with all his strength to lift himself over the edge. But the pan began to climb before he succeeded, leaving him helpless on the lower edge of the incline; and the best he could do to save himself was to cling to it with bare, striving fingers, waiting for his opportunity to renew itself.

To Tommy Lark it was plain that Sandy Rowl could not lift himself out of the water.

"Hang fast!" he shouted. "I'll help you!"

Timing his start, as best he was able, to land him on the pan in the middle of the lane when it lay in the trough, Tommy Lark set out to the rescue. It will be recalled that the pan would not support two men. Two men could not accurately adjust their weight. Both would strive for the center. They would grapple there; and, in the end, when the pan jumped on edge both would be thrown off.

Tommy Lark was aware of the capacity of the pan. Had that capacity been equal to the weight of two men, it would have been a simple matter for him to run out, grasp Sandy Rowl by the collar, and drag him from the water. In the circumstances, however, what help he could give Sandy Rowl must be applied in the moment through which he would remain on the ice before it sank; and enough of the brief interval must be saved wherein to escape either onward or back.

Rowl did not need much help. With one knee on the ice, lifting himself with all his might, a strong, quick pull would assist him over the edge.

But Rowl was not ready. When Tommy Lark landed on the pan, Sandy was deep in the water, his hands gripping the ice, his face upturned, his shoulders submerged. Tommy did not even pause. He ran on to the other side of the lane. When he turned, Rowl had an elbow and foot on the pan and was waiting for help; but Tommy Lark hesitated, disheartened—the pan would support less weight than he had thought.

The second trial failed. Rowl was ready. It was not that. Tommy Lark landed awkwardly on the pan from the fifth cake of ice. He consumed the interval of his stay in regaining his feet. He did not dare remain. Before he could stretch a hand toward Rowl, the pan was submerged, and he must leap on in haste to the opposite shore of the lane; and the escape had been narrow—almost he had been caught.

Returning, then, to try for the third time, he caught Rowl by the collar, jerked him, felt him rise, dropped him, sure that he had contributed the needed impulse, and ran on. But when he turned, confident that he would find Rowl sprawling on the pan, Rowl had failed and dropped back in the water.

For the fourth time Tommy essayed the crossing, with Rowl waiting, as before, foot and elbow on the ice; and he was determined to leap more cautiously from the fifth cake of ice and to risk more on the pan that he might gain more—to land more circumspectly, opposing his weight to Rowl's weight, and to pause until the pan was flooded deep. The plan served his turn. He landed fairly, bent deliberately, caught Rowl's coat with both hands, dragged him on the pan, leaped away, springing out of six inches of water; and when, having crossed to the Scalawag shore of the lane, he turned, Rowl was still on the ice, flat on his back, resting. It was a rescue.

Presently Sandy Rowl joined Tommy Lark.

"All right?" Tommy inquired.

"I'm cold an' I'm drippin'," Sandy replied; "but otherwise I'm fair enough an' glad t' be breathin' the breath o' life. I won't thank you, Tommy."

"I don't want no thanks."

"I won't thank you. No, Tommy. I'll do better. I'll leave Elizabeth t' thank you. You've won a full measure o' thanks, Tommy, from Elizabeth."

"You thinks well o' yourself," Tommy declared. "I'm danged if you don't!"

An hour later Tommy Lark and the dripping Sandy Rowl entered the kitchen of Elizabeth Luke's home at Scalawag Harbor. Skipper James was off to prayer meeting. Elizabeth Luke's mother sat knitting alone by the kitchen fire. To her, then, Tommy Lark presented the telegram, having first warned her, to ease the shock, that a message had arrived, contents unknown, from the region of Grace Harbor. Having commanded her self-possession, Elizabeth Luke's mother received and read the telegram, Tommy Lark and Sandy Rowl standing by, eyes wide to catch the first indication of the contents in the expression of the slow old woman's countenance.

There was no indication, however—not that Tommy Lark and Sandy Rowl could read. Elizabeth Luke's mother stared at the telegram; that was all. She was neither downcast nor rejoiced. Her face was blank.

Having read the brief message once, she read it again; and having reflected, and having read it for the third time, and having reflected once more, without achieving any enlightenment whatsoever, she looked up, her wrinkled face screwed in an effort to solve the mystery. She pursed her lips, she tapped the floor with her toe, she tapped her nose with her forefinger, she pushed up her spectacles, she scratched her chin, even she scratched her head; and then she declared to Tommy Lark and Sandy Rowl that she could make nothing of it at all.

"Is the maid sick?" Tommy inquired.

"She is."

"I knowed it!" Tommy declared.

"She says she's homesick." Elizabeth's mother pulled down her spectacles and referred to the telegram. " 'Homesick,' says she," she added.

"What else?"

"I can't fathom it. I knows what she means

when she says she's homesick; I've been that myself. But what's this about Squid Cove? 'Tis the queerest thing ever I knowed!"

Tommy Lark flushed.

"Woman," he demanded, eager and tense, "what does the maid say about Squid Cove?"

"She says she's homesick for the cottage in Squid Cove. An' that's every last word that she says."

"There's no cottage in Squid Cove," said Sandy.

"No cottage there," Elizabeth's mother agreed, "t' be homesick for. 'Tis a very queer thing."

"There's no cottage in Squid Cove," said Tommy Lark; "but there's lumber for a cottage lyin' there on the rocks."

"What about that?"

"'Tis my lumber!" Tommy roared. "An' the maid knows it!"

II

THE SIREN OF SCALAWAG RUN

II

THE SIREN OF SCALAWAG RUN

SCALAWAG RUN suspected the sentimental entanglement into which Fate had mischievously cast Dickie Blue and pretty Peggie Lacey and there abandoned them; and Scalawag Run was inclined to be more scornful than sympathetic. What Dickie Blue should have done in the circumstances was transparent to every young blade in the harbor—an instant, bold behavior, issuing immediately in the festive popping of guns at a wedding and a hearty charivari thereafter; and those soft devices to which pretty Peggy Lacey should have resorted without scruple in her own relief, were not unknown, you may be sure, to the wise, whispering maids of the place. It was too complacently agreed that the situation, being left to the direction and mastery of Time, would proceed to a happy conclusion as a matter of course. There would be a conjunction of the light of the moon, for example, with the soft, love-lorn weather of June—the shadows of the alders on the winding road to Squid Cove and the sleepy tinkle of the goats' bells dropping down from the slopes of The Topmast into the murmur of the sea. There had been just such favorable auspices of late, however—June moonlight and the music of a languorous night, with Dickie Blue and pretty Peggy Lacey meandering the shadowy Squid Cove road together; and the experience of Scalawag Run was still defied—no blushes and laughter and shining news of a wedding at Scalawag Run.

Dickie Blue, returning from the Squid Cove road, found his father, Skipper John, waiting at the gate.

"Well?" Skipper John demanded.

"'Tis I, sir."

"I knows that. I been waitin' for you. How'd ye get along the night?"

"I got along well enough."

"How far did yer get along?"

"I—I proceeded."

"What did ye do?"

"Who, sir?" Dickie replied. "Me?"

"Ay, you! Who else?"

"I didn't do nothin' much," said Dickie.

"Ha!" Skipper John snorted. "Nothin' much, eh! Was you with the maid at all on the roads?"

"Well, yes, sir," Dickie replied. "I was with her."

Skipper John spoke in scorn. "You was with her!" said he. "An' you didn't do nothin' much! Well, well!" And then, explosively: "Did you do nothin' at all?"

"I didn't go t' no great lengths with her."

"What lengths?"

"Well," Dickie drawled, "I——"

Skipper John broke in impatiently. "What I wants t' know," said he, "is a very simple thing. Did you pop?"

"Me?"

Skipper John was disgusted.

"Ecod!" he ejaculated. "Then you didn't!"

"I didn't pop," said Dickie. "That is—not quite."

"Did you come into peril o' poppin'?"

"Well," Dickie admitted, "I brooded on it."

"Whew!" Skipper John ejaculated. "You brooded on it, did you? An' what happened then?"

"I—I hesitated."

"Well, well! Now that was cautious, wasn't it? An' why did you—hesitate?"

"Dang it!" Dickie complained, "t' hear you talk, a man might think that Peggy Lacey was the only maid in Scalawag Run. I'm willin' an' eager t' be wed. I jus' don't want t' make no mistake. That's all. Dang it, there's shoals o' maids hereabouts! An' I isn't goin' t' swallow the first hook that's cast my way. I'll take my time, sir, an' that's an end o' the matter."

"You're nigh twenty-one," Skipper John warned.

"I've time enough yet. I'm in no hurry."

"Pah!" Skipper John snorted. "'Tis a poor stick of a man that's as slow as you at courtin'! No hurry, eh? What ye made of, anyhow? When I was your age——"

"Have done with boastin', sir. I'll not be driven. I'll pick and choose an' satisfy my taste."

"Is Peggy Lacey a wasteful maid?" Skipper John inquired.

"No; she's not a wasteful maid."

"Is she good?"

"She's pious enough for me."

"Is she healthy?"

"Nothin' wrong with her health that anybody ever fetched t' my notice. She seems sound."

"Is she fair?"

"She'll pass."

"I'm not askin' if she pass. I'm askin' you if she isn't the fairest maid in Scalawag Run."

"'Tis a matter o' taste, father."

"An' what's your taste—if you have any?"

"If I was pickin' a fault," Dickie replied, "I'd say that she might have a touch more o' color in her cheeks t' match my notion o' beauty."

"A bit too pallid t' suit your delicate notion o' beauty!" Skipper John scoffed. "Well, well!"

"I knows rosier maids than she."

"I've no doubt of it. 'Tis a pity the good Lord's handiwork can't be remedied t' suit you. Mm-mm! Well, well! An' is there anything else out o' the way with God Almighty's idea o' what a fair maid looks like?"

"Dang me!" Dickie protested again. "I isn't denyin' that she's fair!"

"No; but——"

"Ah, well, isn't I got a right t' my notions? What's the harm in admirin' rosy cheeks? Isn't nothin' the matter with rosy cheeks, is there?"

"They fade, my son."

"I knows that well enough, sir," Dickie declared; "but they're pretty while they last. An' I'd never be the man t' complain, sir, when they faded. You'd not think so ill o' me as all that, would you?"

"You'd not—complain when they faded?"

"I'd not shame my honor so!"

"Ah, well, Dick," said Skipper John, having reflected a moment upon this fine, honest sentiment, " 'tis not the pallid cheeks o' the maid that trouble you. I knows you well, an' I knows what the trouble is. The maid has been frank enough t' leave you see that she cares for you. She've no wiles to entangle you with; an' I 'low that she'd despise the use o' them anyhow. Did she cast her line with cunnin', she'd hook you soon enough; but that she'll never do, my son—she's too proud an' honest for that. Ay; that's it—too innocent t' conceal her feelin's an' too proud to ensnare you. You was always the lad, Dick, t' scorn what you could have an' crave that which was beyond your reach. Do you mind the time when you took over the little *Robin's Wing* from Trader Tom Jenkins for the Labrador fishin'? She was offered you on fair credit, an' you found fault with the craft an' the terms, an' dawdled an' complained, until Trader Tom offered her t' Long George Long o' Hide-an'-Seek Harbor; an' then you went flyin' t' Trader Tom's office, with your heart in your mouth, lest you lose the chance afore you got there. Had Trader Tom withheld the *Robin's Wing*, you would have clamored your voice hoarse t' get her. Speak me fair, now—is you sorry you took the *Robin's Wing?*"

"I isn't."

"Is you ever repented a minute?"

"No, sir. Why should I?"

"Then there's a hint for your stupidity in that matter. Take the maid an' be done with it. God be thanked I isn't a widower-man. If I was, I'd bring your chance into peril soon enough," said his father. " 'Tis t' be a fair day for fishin' the Skiff-an'-Punt grounds the morrow. Go t' bed. I'll pray that wisdom may overcome your caution afore you're decrepit."

Skipper John thought his son a great dunderhead. And Dickie Blue was a dunderhead. No doubt about it. Yet the failing was largely the fault of his years. A strapping fellow, this young Dickie Blue, blue-eyed in the Newfoundland way, and merry and modest enough in the main, who had recently discovered a critical interest in the comparative charms of the maids of the harbor. There were so many maids in the world! Dang it, it was confusing! There was Peggy Lacey. She was adorable. Nobody could deny it. Had she worn roses in her cheeks she would have been irresistible altogether. And there was the new schoolmistress from Grace Harbor. That superior maid had her points, too. She did not lack attractions. They were more intellectual than anything else. Still, they had a positive appeal. There were snares for the heart in brilliant conversation and a traveled knowledge of the world. Dang it, anyhow, a man might number all the maids in the harbor and find charms enough in each! Only a fool would choose from such an abundance in haste. A wise man would deliberate—observe, compare, reflect; and a sure conviction would come of that course.

Well, now, pretty Peggy Lacey, pretty as she was, was not aggressively disposed. She was a passive, too sanguine little creature; and being limpid and tender as well, and more loyal than artful, she had failed to conceal her ardent attachment and its anxious expectancy. Had she loosed a wink of challenge from her gray eyes in another direction, the reluctance of Dickie Blue might have been reduced with astonishing rapidity, and she could have punished his stupidity at will, had she been maliciously inclined. Conceiving such practices to be both cheap and artful, however, and being, after all, of a pretty sturdy turn of character, she rejected the advantages of deceitful behavior, as she called it, and in consequence lived in a state of cruel uncertainty. Worse than that, she was no longer sought; and for this, too, she was wholly responsible. In a spirit of loyalty to Dickie Blue, who deserved nothing so devoted, she had repelled other advances; and when, once, in a wicked mood of pique, as she afterward determined, she had walked with Sandy Watt on the Squid Cove road, the disloyalty implied, mixed with fear of the consequences, made her too wretched to repeat that lapse from a faithful and consistent conduct. She was quite sure that Dickie Blue would be angered again if she did (he was savagely angry)—that he would be driven away for good and all.

"You must not do it again, Peggy," Dickie Blue had admonished. "Now, mind what I'm tellin' you!"

"I won't," the soft little Peggy promised in haste.

"Now, that's sensible," said Dickie Blue. He was in earnest. And his purpose was high.

"Still an' all," Peggy began, "there's no harm——"

"What does a maid know about that?" Dickie interrupted. "It takes a man t' know a man. The lad's not fit company for the likes o' you." It was true. "You must look upon me, Peggy, as an elder brother, an' be guided by my advice. I'll watch over you, Peggy, jus' as well as an elder brother can."

"I'm grateful," Peggy murmured, flushed with pleasure in this interest. "I thanks you."

"There's no call t' thank me," Dickie protested. "'Tis a pleasure t' serve you."

"Thank you," said Peggy.

Skipper John Blue was a hearty old codger. Pretty Peggy Lacey, whose father had been cast away in the *Sink or Swim,* long ago, on the reefs off Thumb-an'-Finger of the Labrador, loved and used him like a father and found him sufficient to her need. To pretty Peggy Lacey, then, Skipper John cautiously repeated the substance of his conversation with Dickie Blue, adding a whisper of artful advice and a chuckle of delight in it. Peggy Lacey was appalled by the deceitful practice disclosed by Skipper John, whose sophistication she suspected and deplored. She had no notion at all, said she, that such evil as he described could walk abroad and unshamed in the good world, and she wondered what old mischief of his youth had informed him; and she would die a maid, loveless and childless, she declared, rather than have the guilt of a deception of such magnitude on her soul. Moreover, where were the means to be procured for executing the enormity? There was nothing of the sort, she was sure, in Trader Tom Jenkins's shop at Scalawag Run. There was nothing of the sort to be had anywhere short of St. John's; and as for sanctioning a plan so bold as sending a letter and a post-office order to Skipper John's old friend in St. John's, the lively widow o' the late Cap'n Saul Nash, o' the *Royal Bloodhound,* pretty Peggy Lacey jus' pos'tively would not do no such thing.

Skipper John found his head convenient to assist the expression of his emotion. He scratched it.

"Well, I'm bewildered," said he, "an' I'm not able t' help you at all no more."

"I'll have nobody's help," Peggy Lacey retorted.

"Why not, Peggy?"

"I've my pride t' serve."

"My dear," said Skipper John gravely, "you've also your happiness t' gain."

"I'll gain it alone."

"Aw, now, Peggy," Skipper John coaxed, with a forefinger under Peggy's little chin, "you'd take my help in this an' in all things, wouldn't ye? You is jus' so used t' my help, maid," he added, "that you'd be wonderful lonesome without it."

That was true.

"In most things, Father John," Peggy replied, "I'd take your help an' be glad. Whatever an' all about that, I'll have nobody's help in the world t' win the mastery o' Dickie Blue. Mark that, now! I means it."

"I've showed you the way t' win it."

" 'Tis dishonest."

"Ay, but——"

" 'Tis shameful."

"Still an' all——"

"I'll not do it."

Again Skipper John scratched his head. " 'Tis an old sayin'," he protested, "that all's fair in love an' war."

" 'Tis a false sayin'," Peggy declared. "Moreover," she argued, "an I took your advice, an' done the schemin' wickedness that you said, 'twould never win Dickie Blue."

"Jus' you try it, maid!"

"I scorn t' try it! I'll practice no wiles whatsoever t' win the likes o' Dickie Blue. An' what would I say when he discovered the deception thereafter?"

"He'd never find out at all."

"Sure, he've eyes t' see with, haven't he?"

"Ay, but he's too stupid t' notice. An' once you're wed——"

"No, no! 'Tis a thing too awful t' plot."

"An you cared enough for the lad," said Skipper John, "you'd stop at nothin' at all."

Peggy's great eyes clouded with tears.

"I cares more for he," said she, "than he cares for me. My heart's jus' sore with grief."

"Ah, no, now!"

"Ay, 'tis!" Peggy sobbed. She put her dark hair against Skipper John's shoulder then. "I'm jus' sick with the need of un!" she said.

Summer went her indifferent way, and Winter blustered into the past, too, without serving the emotions of Scalawag Run; and a new Spring was imminent—warm winds blowing out of the south, the ice breaking from the cliffs and drifting out to sea and back again. Still pretty Peggy Lacey was obdurately fixed in her attitude toward the sly suggestion of Skipper John Blue. Suffer she did—that deeply; but she sighed in secret and husbanded her patience with what stoicism she could command. There were times, twilight falling on the world of sea and rock beyond the kitchen window, with the last fire of the sun failing in the west like a bright hope—there were hours when her fear of the issue was so poignant that her decision trembled. The weather mellowed; the temptation gathered strength and renewed itself persistently—the temptation discreetly to accept the aid of artifice. After all, what matter? 'Twas surely a thing o' small consequence. An' who would ever hear the least whisper about it? For a long time Peggy Lacey rejected the eager promptings of her love—clenched her little red fists and called her pride to the rescue; and then, all at once, of a yellow day, having chanced to glance out of the window and down the harbor in the direction of Cottage Point, and having clapped eyes on a sight that pinched and shook the very heart of her, she was changed in a twinkling into the Siren of Scalawag Run.

Peggy Lacey sped forthwith to Skipper John, whom she found alone in his kitchen, oiling his sealing-gun.

"Father John," she demanded, "what's all this I sees goin' on on the tip o' Cottage Point?"

Skipper John glanced out of the wide kitchen window.

"Ah," said he, "that's on'y young Dickie at labor.

He've selected that pretty spot an' is haulin' his lumber afore the snow's gone."

"Haulin' his lumber?" Peggy gasped.

"Mm-m."

"Haulin' l-l-lumber!"

"Mm-m. I sees he've ol' Tog in harness with the rest o' the dogs. Well, well! Tog's too old for that labor."

"Who's the maid?"

"Maid!"

"What's he haulin' lumber for?"

"I 'low he's haulin' lumber jus' for the same reason that any young fellow would haul lumber for in the Spring o' the year."

" 'Tis a new house, isn't it?"

"Ay; 'tis a new house. He've been plannin' t' build his house this long time, as you knows very well, an' now he've gone at it in a forehanded way."

"Well, then," Peggy insisted, finding it hard to command breath for the question, "who's the maid?"

"No maid in particular that I knows of."

"Well, I knows!" Peggy flashed. " 'Tis the new schoolmistress from Grace Harbor. That's who 'tis!"

"Ah-ha!" said Skipper John.

"Yes, 'tis! She've cotched his fancy with her eyeglasses an' grammar. The false, simperin', titterin' cat! Oh, poor Dickie Blue!"

"Whew!"

"She'd never do for un, Skipper John."

"No?"

"Never. They're not suited to each other at all. He'd be mis'able with her."

Skipper John grinned.

"Poor Dickie!" he sighed.

Peggy Lacey was in tears at last.

"Father John," she sobbed, "I'm jus' desperate with fear an' grief. I can't bear it no longer." She began to pace the floor in a tumult of emotion. "I can't breathe," said she. "I'm stifled. My heart's like t' burst with pain." She paused—she turned to Skipper John, swaying where she stood, her hands pitifully reaching toward the old man, her face gray and dull with the agony she could no longer endure; and her eyes closed, and her head dropped, and her voice fell to a broken whisper. "Oh, hold me!" she entreated. "I'm sick. I'll fall."

Skipper John took her in his arms.

"Ah, hush!" he crooned. "'Tis not so bad as all that. An' he's not worth it, the great dunderhead!"

Peggy Lacey pushed Skipper John away.

"I'll not yield t' nobody!" she stormed, her soft little face gone hard with a savage determination. Her red little lips curled and the nostrils of her saucy little nose contemptuously expanded. "I've neither eye-glasses nor grammar," said she, "but I'll ensnare Dickie Blue for all that."

"I would," said Skipper John.

"I will!"

"An' without scruple!"

"Not a twinge!"

"I'd have no mercy."

"Not I!"

"An' I'd encourage no delay."

"Skipper John, do you write that letter t' St. John's this very day," said Peggy, her soft, slender little body magnificently drawn up to the best of its alluring inches. She snapped, "We'll see what comes o' that!"

"Hoosh!" Skipper John gloated.

"Waste no time, sir. 'Tis a ticklish matter."

"The answer will be shipped straight t' you, Peggy. 'Twill be here in less 'n a fortnight." Skipper John broke into a wild guffaw of laughter. "An' Dickie himself will fetch the trap for his own feet, ecod!"

Peggy remained grave.

"I'm determined," she declared. "There's nothin' will stop me now. I'll do it, no matter what."

"Well, then," said Skipper John, "I 'low 'tis all over but the weddin'."

Skipper John privately thought, after all, that a good deal of fuss was being made over the likes o' Dickie Blue. And I think so too. However, the affair was Peggy Lacey's. And doubtless she knew her own business well enough to manage it without ignorant criticism.

In the Winter weather, when the coast was locked in with ice, and continuing until the first cruise of the mail-boat in May, to be precise, Dickie Blue carried his Majesty's mail, once a fortnight, by government contract, from the railroad at Bottom Harbor to Scalawag Run and all the harbors of Whale Bay. It was inevitable, therefore, that he should be aware of the communication addressed to Miss Peggy Lacey of Scalawag Run; and acutely aware of it he was—the communication and the little box that seemed to accompany it. From Bottom Harbor to All-in-the-Way Island, he reflected occasionally upon the singular circumstance. Who had sent a gift to Peggy Lacey from St. John's? Could it have been Charlie Rush? Charlie Rush was in St. John's to ship for the ice with the sealing fleet. Pausing on the crest of Black Cliff to survey the crossing to Scalawag Run, he came to a conclusion in relation to Peggy Lacey's letter that was not at all flattering to his self-esteem.

The letter mystified Dickie Blue—the author of the communication; but he had no difficulty in surmising the contents of the box to his own satisfaction.

"'Tis a ring," he determined.

By that time the day was near spent. Dusk would fall within the hour. Already the wide flare of light above the wilderness had failed to the dying ashes of its fire. Prudence urged a return to the cottage at Point-o'-Bay Cove for the night. True, it was not far from Black Cliff across the run to the first rocks of Scalawag. It was short of a mile, at any rate. Dickie could glimpse the lights of the Scalawag hills—the folk were lighting the lamps in the kitchens; and he fixed his eyes on Peggy Lacey's light, in the yellow glow of which, no doubt, pretty Peggy was daintily busied with making a supper of no dainty proportions; and he cocked his head and scowled in deliberation, and he stood irresolute on the brink of the cliff, playing with the temptation to descend and cross, as though a whiff from Peggy Lacey's kitchen stove had invited and challenged him over. It was not so much the visionary whiff of Peggy Lacey's supper, however, that challenged his courage: it was Peggy Lacey's letter in the pack on his back, and Peggy Lacey's suggestive packet, that tantalized him to reckless behavior. Ah-ha, he'd show Peggy Lacey what it was to carry the mail in a way that a man should carry it! He'd put the love-letter an' the ring in her hand forthwith. His Majesty's mail would go through that night.

"Ha!" he gloated. "I'll further her courtship. An' that'll settle her, ecod! I'll show her once an' for all that 'tis no matter t' me whom she weds."

There were stout reasons, however, against attempting to cross the run that night. The lane was filled from shore to shore with fragments of ice. Moreover, fog was blowing in from the east in the wake of the departing day, and rain threatened—a cold drizzle. All this being patent, the rain and peril of the passage in contrast with the dry, lighted kitchens of Point-o'-Bay Cove, Dickie Blue crossed Scalawag Run that night notwithstanding; and the mere circumstance of the crossing, where was no haste that he knew of, indicated at least the perturbation of his emotions. Well, Peggy Lacey might wed whom she pleased, an' he'd further her schemes, too, at the risk of his life. She should have her letter at once—her ring without delay; an' as for Dickie Blue, 'twas a closed book of romance—there were other maids at Scalawag Run, fairer maids, more intellectual maids, an' he'd love one o' them soon enough.

When Dickie Blue entered, Skipper John looked up, amazed.

"Did ye cross the run this night?" said he.

"I'll leave you, sir," Dickie answered curtly, "t' solve that deep riddle for yourself. You'll not be needing my help."

Skipper John reflected.

"Was there a letter for Peggy Lacey?" said he. "She've been eager for a message from St. John's."

"There was."

"Nothin' else, I 'low?"

"There was. There was a packet."

"Whew!" Skipper John ejaculated. "That's a pity. I been fearin' an outcome o' that sort. An

I was you, Dick," he advised, "I'd lose no time in that direction."

" 'Tis not my purpose to."

"Ye'll wed the maid?"

"I will not."

"Ye obstinate dunderhead!" Skipper John scolded. "I believes ye! Dang if I don't! Go to! Shift them wet clothes, sir, an' come t' supper. I hopes a shrew hooks ye. Dang if I don't!"

In gloomy perturbation, in ill humor with the daft dealings of the world he lived in, Dickie Blue left the soggy road and sad drizzle of the night for the warm, yellow light of Peggy Lacey's kitchen, where pretty Peggy, alone in the housewifely operation, was stowing the clean dishes away. Yet his course was shaped—his reflections were determined; and whatever Peggy Lacey might think to the contrary, as he was no better, after all, than a great, blundering, obstinate young male creature, swayed by vanity and pique, and captive of both in that crisis, Peggy Lacey's happiness was in a desperate situation. It was farther away at the moment of Dickie Blue's sullen entrance than ever it had been since first she flushed and shone with the vision of its glorious approach.

Ay—thought the perverse Dickie Blue when he clapped eyes on the fresh gingham in which Peggy Lacey was fluttering over the kitchen floor (he would not deign to look in her gray eyes), the maid might have her letter an' her ring an' wed whom she pleased; an' as for tears at the weddin', they'd not fall from the eyes o' Dickie Blue, who would by that time, ecod, perhaps have consummated an affair with a maid of consequence from Grace Harbor! Ha! There were indeed others! The charms of the intellect were not negligible. They were to be taken into account in the estimate. And Dickie Blue would consider the maid from Grace Harbor.

"She've dignity," thought he, "an' she've learnin'. Moreover, she've high connections in St. John's an' a wonderful complexion."

Dickie meant it. Ay. And many a man, and many a poor maid, too, as everybody knows, has cast happiness to waste in a mood of that mad description. And so a tragedy impended.

"Is it you, Dick?" says Peggy Lacey.

Dickie nodded and scowled.

"'Tis I. Was you lookin' for somebody else t' call?"

"No, Dickie."

It was almost an interrogation. Peggy Lacey was puzzled. Dickie Blue's gloomy concern was out of the way.

"Well," said Dicky, "I'm sorry."

"An' why?"

"Well," Dickie declared, "if you was expectin' anybody else t' come t' see you, I'd be glad t' have un do so. 'Tis a dismal evenin' for you t' spend alone."

Almost, then, Peggy Lacey's resolution failed her. Almost she protested that she would have a welcome for no other man in the world. Instead she turned arch.

"Did you bring the mail?" she inquired.

"I did."

"Was there nothin' for me?"

"There was."

"A letter!"

"Ay."

Peggy Lacey trembled. Confronting, thus intimately, the enormity she proposed, she was shocked. She concealed her agitation, however, and laid strong hands upon her wicked resolution to restrain its flight.

"Nothin' else?" said she.

"Ay; there was more."

"Not a small packet!"

"Ay; there was a small packet. I 'low you been expectin' some such gift as that, isn't you?"

"A gift! Is it from St. John's?"

"Ay."

"Then I been expectin' it," Peggy eagerly admitted. "Where is it, Dickie? I'm in haste to pry into that packet."

The letter and the package were handed over.

"'Tis not hard," said Dickie, "t' guess the contents of a wee box like that. I could surmise them myself."

Peggy started.

"Wh-wh-what!" she ejaculated. "You know the contents! Oh, dear me!"

"No, I don't know the contents. I could guess them, though, an I had a mind to."

"You never could guess. 'Tis not in the mind of a man t' fathom such a thing as that. There's a woman's secret in this wee box."

" 'Tis a ring."

"A ring!" Peggy challenged. "You'd not care, Dickie Blue, an 'twas a ring t' betroth me!"

Dickie Blue was sure that his surmise had gone cunningly to its mark. Pride flashed to the rescue of his self-esteem. His face flared. He rose in wrath.

"Betrothed, is you?" he flung out. "I'll weather it, maid! Ha! I'll weather it!"

"Weather it!" cried poor Peggy, in a flame of indignation.

"I'm not hurt!"

"Sit you down!"

"I'll not sit down. I'm goin'."

"Sit you down, oaf that you is!" Peggy Lacey commanded. "I'll read my letter an' open my packet an' return. Don't ye budge! Don't ye dare!"

Peggy Lacey swept out of the kitchen. Her head was high. There was no compassion in her heart. Nor was she restrained by any lingering fear of the consequences of that wicked deceit to the immediate practice of which she had committed herself. And as for Dickie Blue, he sat stock-still where she had bade him remain, his eyes wide with the surprise of the domination. He did not budge. He did not dare.

Precisely what Peggy Lacey did in the seclusion of her chamber it would be indelicate to disclose. Moreover, I am not minutely aware of all the intricacies of the employment of those mysterious means by which she accomplished the charming effect that she did in some intuitive way presently accomplish; and at any rate I decline the task of description. I confess, however, that the little packet contained a modest modicum of the necessary materials, whatever they were; and I have no hesitation in praising the generous interest, the discretion and exuberant experience of the gay widow of the late Cap'n Saul Nash o' the *Royal Bloodhound,* whose letter, dealing with the most satisfactory methods of application, as related to the materials aforesaid, whatever they were, and whose wisdom included a happy warning or two—I have no hesitation in admitting that the letter was completely sufficient to enlighten the ignorance of pretty Peggy Lacey, and to steel her resolution and to guide her unreluctant hand in its deceitful work. When at last she stood back from the mirror to survey and appraise the result, she dimpled with delight. It was ravishing, no doubt about that! It supplied the only lack of which the disclosure of sly old Skipper John had informed her. And she tossed her dark head in a proper saucy fashion, and she touched a strand of hair to deliberate disarray, and smoothed her apron; and then she tripped into the kitchen to exercise the wiles of the little siren that she had become.

"I've cast my everlastin' soul into the balance," poor Peggy accused herself, "an' I don't care a whit!"

All this while Dickie Blue had occupied himself with more reasonable reflection than he was accustomed to entertain. Doubt alarmed him. Betrothed, was she? Well, she might be betrothed an she wanted to! Who cared? Still an' all—well, she was young t' be wed, wasn't she? An' she had no discretion in choice. Poor wee thing, she had given herself t' some wastrel, no doubt! Charlie Rush! Ecod! Huh! 'Twas a poor match for a dear maid like she t' make. An' Dickie Blue would miss her sadly when she was wed away from his care an' affection. Affection? Ay; he was wonderful fond o' the pallid wee thing. 'Twas a pity she had no color—no blushes t' match an' assist the roguish loveliness o' the big eyes that was forever near trappin' the heart of a man. Dang it, she was fair anyhow! What was rosy cheeks, after all. They faded like roses. Ah, she was a wonderful dear wee thing! 'Twas a melancholy pity that she was t' be wed so young. Not yet seventeen! Mm-m—'twas far too young. Dang it, Charlie Rush would be home afore long with the means in his pocket for a weddin'! Dang it, they'd be wed when he come! An' then pretty Peggy Lacey would no longer be——

When Peggy Lacey tripped into the kitchen, Dickie Blue was melancholy with the fear that she was more dear than he had known.

"Peggy!" he gasped.

Then he succumbed utterly. She was radiant. Roses? They bloomed in her round cheeks! Dear Lord, what full-blown flowers they were! Dickie Blue went daft with love of Peggy Lacey. No caution now! A flame of love and devotion! Splendor clothed the boy.

"What ails you?" said Peggy defiantly. "You is starin' at me most rudely."

Dickie Blue's mounting love thrilled and troubled him with a protective concern.

"You isn't ill, is you?" he demanded.

"Ill!" she scoffed. "I never felt better in all my life. An' why d'ye ask me that?"

"You're flushed."

"I'm sorry," she replied demurely, "that you've a distaste for the color in my cheeks. I wish I might be able t' rub it off t' suit ye."

He smiled.

"I never seed ye so rosy afore," said he. "You're jus' bloomin' like a flower, Peggy."

"Ah, well," the mendacious little creature replied, with an indifferent shrug of her soft shoulders, "mostly I'm not rosy at all, but there's days when I is. I'm sorry you're offended by rosy cheeks like mine. I'll try not t' have it happen again when you're about."

"I'm not offended, Peggy."

There was that in Dickie Blue's voice to make Peggy Lacey's heart flutter.

"No?" says she.

"Far from it."

"I—I'm s'prised!"

"You—you is jus' beautiful the night, Peggy!"

"The night?"

"An' always was an' always will be!"

"I can't believe ye think it."

Dickie Blue went close to Peggy then. "Peggy," said he, "was there a ring in the wee box I fetched you the night?"

"No, sir."

"Is you betrothed, Peggy?"

Peggy dropped her head to hide the tears. She was more afraid than ever. Yet she must listen, she knew, and reply with courage and truth.

"I—I'm not," she faltered.

"God be thanked!" said Dickie Blue. "Ah, Peggy, Peggy," he whispered, "I loves you!"

"You mustn't say it, Dickie!"

"I can't help myself."

All at once Peggy Lacey's conscience submerged

her spirit in a flood of reproaches. There was no maid more false in all the world, she knew, than her own wicked self.

"Dickie," she began, "I—I——"

"Has you no word o' love for me, Peggy? I—I jus' crave it, Peggy, with all my heart. Yes, I do!"

"Stay jus' where you is!" Peggy sobbed. "Don't you budge a inch, Dickie! I'll be back in a minute."

With that she fled. She vanished, indeed, in full flight, into that chamber whence she had issued radiantly rosy a few moments before, once more abandoning Dickie Blue to an interval of salutary reflection. To intrude in pursuit, of course—for the whole troop of us to intrude, curious and gaping, upon those swift measures which Peggy Lacey was impetuously executing in relief of the shafts of her accusing conscience—would be a breach of manners too gross even to contemplate; but something may be inferred from a significant confusion of sounds which the closed door failed altogether to conceal. There was clink of pitcher and basin; there was a great splash of water, as of water being poured with no caution to confine it to the receptacle provided to receive it; there was the thump of a pitcher on the floor; and there was more splashing, then a violent agitation, and the trickle and drip of water, and a second and a third violent agitation of the liquid contents of what appeared to be a porcelain bowl—the whole indicating that the occupant of the chamber was washing her face in haste with a contrite determination to make a thorough success of the ablution. And there was silence, broken by gasps and stifled sobs—doubtless a vigorous rubbing was in course; and then the door was flung open from within, and Peggy Lacey dashed resolutely in the direction of the kitchen.

A moment later Peggy Lacey confronted Dickie Blue. She was reckless; she was defiant. She was tense; she was piercing.

"Look at me!" she commanded.

Dickie Blue was mild and smiling. "I'm lookin'," said he. "I can look no other where."

"Is you lookin' close?"

"Ay. My look's hungry for the sight o' your dear face. I'm blind with admiration. I wants t' gaze forever."

"Where's my roses now?"

"They've fled. What matter?"

"Ay—fled! An' where?"

"They've retreated whence they came so prettily. 'Tis a lure o' that sweet color t' come an' go."

Peggy gasped.

"Whence they came!" she faltered. "Ah, where did they come from, Dickie? Don't ye know?"

"A while gone you was flushed with a pretty modesty," Dickie replied, smiling indulgent explanation, "an' now you is pale with a sad fright at my rough love-makin'."

"I'm not frightened at all. Look at my nose!"

" 'Tis the sauciest little knob in the world!"

"Look with care. Count 'em!"

"Count what?"

"There's three freckles on it."

"Ay?"

"An' a half."

"Is it so?"

"There, now! I've told you the truth. I'm pallid. I'm freckled. What d'ye think o' me now?"

"I loves you."

"You don't love me at all. You're quite mistaken. You don't know what you're sayin'."

Dickie was bewildered.

"What's all this pother, Peggy?" he pleaded. "I don't know what you're drivin' at, at all."

"I'm pallid again, isn't I?"

"What matter?" said Dickie. "Ah, Peggy, dear," he protested softly, as he advanced, glowing, upon the trembling little maid before him, "all I knows is that I loves you! Will you wed me?"

Peggy Lacey yielded to his embrace. She subsided there in peace. It was safe harbor, she knew; and she longed never to leave its endearing shelter.

"Yes, sir," she whispered.

At that moment Dickie Blue was the happiest man in the world. And he ought to have been, too! Dang me if he shouldn't! And as for Peggy Lacey, she was the happiest maid in the world, which is somewhat surprising, I confess—never so happy as when, before she sought sleep to escape the sweet agony of her joy, she flung the widow Nash's wicked little box of rouge into the driving darkness and heard it splash in the harbor below her chamber window.

III

THE ART OF TERRY LUTE

III

THE ART OF TERRY LUTE

WHEN the *Stand By* went down in a north-easterly gale off Dusty Reef of the False Frenchman, the last example of the art of Terry Lute of Out-of-the-Way Tickle perished with her. It was a great picture. This is an amazing thing to say. It doubtless challenges a superior incredulity. Yet the last example of the art of Terry Lute was a very great picture. Incredible? Not at all. It is merely astonishing. Other masters, and of all sorts, have emerged from obscure places. It is not the less likely that Terry Lute was a master because he originated at Out-of-the-Way Tickle of the Newfoundland north coast. Rather more so, perhaps. At any rate, Terry Lute *was* a master.

James Cobden saw the picture. He, too, was astounded. But—"It is the work of a master," said he, instantly.

Of course the picture is gone; there is no other: Cobden's word for its quality must be taken. But why not? Cobden's judgments are not generally gainsaid; they prove themselves, and stand. And it is not anywhere contended that Cobden is given to the encouragement of anæmic aspiration. Cobden's errors, if any, have been of severity. It is maintained by those who do not love him that he has laughed many a promising youngster into a sour obscurity. And this may be true. A niggard in respect to praise, a skeptic in respect to promise, he is well known. But what he has commended has never failed of a good measure of critical recognition in the end. And he has uncovered no mares'-nests.

All this, however,—the matter of Cobden's authority,—is here a waste discussion. If Cobden's judgments are in the main detestable, the tale has no point for folk of the taste to hold against them; if they are true and agreeable, it must then be believed upon his word that when the *Stand By* went down off Dusty Reef of the False Frenchman a great picture perished with her—a great picture done in crayon on manila paper in Tom Lute's kitchen at Out-of-the-Way Tickle. Cobden is committed to this. And whether a masterpiece or not, and aside from the eminent critical opinion of it, the tale of Terry Lute's last example will at least prove the once engaging quality of Terry Lute's art.

Cobden first saw the picture in the cabin of the *Stand By*, being then bound from Twillingate Harbor to Out-of-the-Way, when in the exercise of an amiable hospitality Skipper Tom took him below to stow him away. Cobden had come sketching. He had gone north, having read some moving and tragical tale of those parts, to look upon a grim sea and a harsh coast. He had found both, and had been inspired to convey a consciousness of both to a gentler world, touched with his own philosophy, in Cobden's way. But here already, gravely confronting him, was a masterpiece greater than he had visioned. It was framed broadly in raw pine, covered with window-glass, and nailed to the bulkhead; but it was nevertheless there, declaring its own dignity, a work of sure, clean genius.

Cobden started. He was astounded, fairly dazed, he puts it, by the display of crude power. He went close, stared into the appalling depths of wind, mist, and the sea, backed off, cocked his astonished head, ran a lean hand in bewilderment through his gray curls, and then flashed about on Skipper Tom.

"Who did that?" he demanded.

"That?" the skipper chuckled. "Oh," he drawled, "jus' my young feller." He was apologetic; but he was yet, to be sure, cherishing a bashful pride.

"How young?" Cobden snapped.

" 'Long about fourteen when he done that."

"A child!" Cobden gasped.

"Well, no, sir," the skipper declared, somewhat

puzzled by Cobden's agitation; "he was fourteen, an' a lusty lad for his years."

Cobden turned again to the picture; he stood in a frowning study of it.

"What's up?" the skipper mildly asked.

"What's up, eh?" says Cobden, grimly. "That's a great picture, by heaven!" he cried. *"That's* what's up."

Skipper Tom laughed.

"She isn't so bad, is she?" he admitted, with interest. "She sort o' scares me by times. But she were meant t' do that. An' dang if I isn't fond of her, anyhow!"

"Show me another," says Cobden.

Skipper Tom sharply withdrew his interest from the picture.

"Isn't another," said he, curtly. "That was the last he done."

"Dead!" Cobden exclaimed, aghast.

"Dead?" the skipper marveled. "Sure, no. He've gone an' growed up." He was then bewildered by Cobden's relief.

Cobden faced the skipper squarely. He surveyed the genial fellow with curious interest.

"Skipper Tom," said he, then, slowly, "you have a wonderful son." He paused. "A—wonderful—son," he repeated. He smiled; the inscrutable wonder of the thing had all at once gently amused him—the wonder that a genius of rarely exampled quality should have entered the world in the neighborhood of Out-of-the-Way Tickle, there abandoned to chance discovery of the most precarious sort. And there was no doubt about the quality of the genius. The picture proclaimed it; and the picture was not promise, but a finished work, in itself an achievement, most marvelously accomplished, moreover, without the aid of any tradition.

Terry Lute's art was triumphant. Even the skeptical Cobden, who had damned so much in his day, could not question the lad's mastery. It did not occur to him to question it.

Skipper Tom blinked at the painter's wistful gravity. "What's the row?" he stammered.

Cobden laughed heartily.

"It is hard to speak in a measured way of all this," he went on, all at once grave again. "After all, perhaps, one guesses; and even the most cautious guesses go awry. I must not say too much. It is not the time, at any rate, to say much. Afterward, when I have spoken with this—this young master, then, perhaps. But I may surely say that the fame of Terry Lute will soon be very great." His voice rose; he spoke with intense emphasis. "It will continue, it will grow. Terry Lute's name will live"—he hesitated—"for generations." He paused now, still looking into the skipper's inquiring eyes, his own smiling wistfully. Dreams were already forming. "Skipper Tom," he added, turning away, "you have a wonderful son."

"Ay," said the skipper, brows drawn; "an' I knows it well enough." He added absently, with deep feeling, "He've been—*jus' fair wonderful.*"

"He shall learn what I can teach him."

"In the way o' sketchin' off, sir?" There was quick alarm in this.

Cobden struck a little attitude. It seemed to him now to be a moment. He was profoundly moved. "Terry Lute," he replied, "shall be—a master!"

"Mr. Cobden, sir," Skipper Tom protested, his face in an anxious twist, "I'll thank you t' leave un alone."

"I'll make a man of him!" cried Cobden, grieved.

Skipper Tom smiled grimly. It was now his turn to venture a curious survey. He ran his eye over the painter's slight body with twinkling amusement. "Will you, now?" he mused. "Oh, well, now," he drawled, "I'd not trouble t' do it an I was you. You're not knowin', anyhow, that he've not made a man of *hisself*. 'Tis five year' since he done that there damned sketch." Then uneasily, and with a touch of sullen resentment: "I 'low you'd best leave un alone, sir. He've had trouble enough as it is."

"So?" Cobden flashed. "Already? That's *good.*"

"It haven't done no harm," the skipper deliberated; "but—well, God knows I'd not like t' see another young one cast away in a mess like that."

Cobden was vaguely concerned. He did not, however, at the moment inquire. It crossed his mind, in a mere flash, that Skipper Tom had spoken with a deal of feeling. What could this trouble have been? Cobden forgot, then, that there had been any trouble at all.

"Well, well," Skipper Tom declared more heartily, "trouble's the foe o' folly."

Cobden laughed pleasantly and turned once more to the picture. He was presently absorbed in a critical ecstasy. Skipper Tom, too, was by this time staring out upon the pictured sea, as though it lay in fearsome truth before him. He was frowning heavily.

It was the picture of a breaker, a savage thing. In the foreground, lifted somewhat from the turmoil, was a black rock. It was a precarious foothold, a place to shrink from in terror. The sea reached for it; the greater waves boiled over and sucked it bare. It was wet, slimy, overhanging death. Beyond the brink was a swirl of broken water—a spent breaker, crashing in, streaked with irresistible current and flecked with hissing fragments.

Adjectives which connote noise are unavoidable. Cobden has said that the picture expressed a sounding confusion. It was true. "You could *hear* that water," says he, tritely. There was the illusion of noise—of the thud and swish of breaking water and of the gallop of the wind. So complete was the illusion, and so did the spirit of the scene transport the beholder, that Cobden once lifted his voice above the pictured tumult. Terry Lute's art was indeed triumphant!

A foreground, then, of slimy rock, an appalling nearness and an inspiration of terror in the swirling breaker below. But not yet the point of dreadful interest. That lay a little beyond. It was a black ledge and a wave. The ledge still dripped the froth of a deluge which had broken and swept on, and there was now poised above it, black, frothy-crested, mightily descending, another wave of the vast and inimical restlessness of the sea beyond.

There was a cliff in the mist above; it was a mere suggestion, a gray patch, but yet a towering wall, implacably there, its presence disclosed by a shadow where the mist had thinned. Fog had broken over the cliff and was streaming down with the wind. Obscurity was imminent; but light yet came from the west, escaping low and clean. And there was a weltering expanse of sea beyond the immediate turmoil; and far off, a streak of white, was the offshore ice.

It was not a picture done in gigantic terms. It was not a climax. Greater winds have blown; greater seas have come tumbling in on the black rocks of Out-of-the-Way. The point is this, Cobden says, that the wind was rising, the sea working up, the ice running in, the fog spreading, thickening, obscuring the way to harbor. The imagination of the beholder was subtly stimulated to conceive the ultimate worst of that which might impend, which is the climax of fear.

Cobden turned to Skipper Tom.

"What does Terry Lute call it?" he asked.

"Nothin'."

"H-m-m!" Cobden deliberated. "It must bear a name. A great picture done by a great hand. It must bear a name."

"Terry calls it jus' 'My Picture.' "

"Let it be called 'The Fang,' " said Cobden.

"A very good name, ecod!" cried Skipper Tom. " 'Tis a picture meant t' scare the beholder."

Terry Lute was not quite shamelessly given to the practice of "wieldin' a pencil" until he discovered that he could make folk laugh. After that he was an abandoned soul, with a naughty strut on the roads. For folk laughed with flattering amazement, and they clapped Terry Lute on his broad little back, and much to his delight they called him a limb o' the devil, and they spread his fame and his sketches from Out-of-the-Way and Twillingate Long Point to Cape Norman and the harbors of the Labrador. Caricatures, of course, engaged him—the parson, the schoolmaster, Bloody Bill Bull, and the crusty old shopkeeper. And had a man an enemy, Terry Lute, at the price of a clap on the back and an admiring wink, would provide him with a sketch which was like an arrow in his hand. The wink of admiration must be above suspicion, however, else Terry's cleverness might take another direction.

By these saucy sketches, Terry Lute was at one period involved in gravest trouble: the schoolmaster, good doctor of the wayward, thrashed him for a rogue; and from a prophetic pulpit the parson, anxious shepherd, came as near to promising him a part in perdition as honest conviction could bring him to speak. Terry Lute was startled. In the weakness of contrition he was moved to promise that he would draw their faces no more, and thereafter he confined his shafts of humor to their backs; but as most men are vulnerable to ridicule from behind, and as the schoolmaster had bandy legs and the parson meek feet and pious shoulders, Terry Lute's pencil was more diligently, and far more successfully, employed than ever. The illicit exercise, the slyer art, and the larger triumph, filled him with chuckles and winks.

"Ecod!" he laughed to his own soul; "you is a sure-enough, clever little marvel, Terry Lute, me b'y!"

What gave Terry Lute's art a profound turn was the sheer indolence of his temperamental breed. He had no liking at all for labor: spreading fish on the flakes, keeping the head of his father's punt up to the sea on the grounds, splitting a turn of birch and drawing a bucket of water from the well by the Needle, discouraged the joy of life. He scolded, he begged, he protested that he was ailing, and so behaved in the cleverest fashion; but nothing availed him until after hours of toil he achieved a woeful picture of a little lad at work on the flake at the close of day. It was Terry Lute himself, no doubt of it at all, but a sad, worn child, with a lame back, eyes of woe, gigantic tears—a tender young spirit oppressed, and, that there might be no mistake about the delicacy of his general health, an angel waiting overhead.

"Thomas," wept Terry Lute's mother, "the wee lad's doomed."

"Hut!" Skipper Tom blurted.

"Shame t' you!" cried Terry's mother, bursting into a new flood of tears.

After that, for a season, Terry Lute ran footloose and joyous over the mossy hills of Out-of-the-Way.

"Clever b'y, Terry Lute!" thinks he, without a qualm.

It chanced by and by that Parson Down preached with peculiar power at the winter revival; and upon this preaching old Bill Bull, the atheist of Out-of-the-Way, attended with scoffing regularity, sitting in the seat of the scorner. It was observed presently—no eyes so keen for such weather as the eyes of Out-of-the-Way—that Bill Bull was coming under conviction of his conscience; and when this great news got abroad, Terry Lute, too, attended upon Parson Down's preaching with regularity, due wholly, however, to his interest in watching the tortured countenance of poor Bill Bull. It was his purpose when first he began to draw to caricature the vanquished wretch. In the end he attempted a moving portrayal of "The Atheist's Stricken State," a large conception.

It was a sacred project; it was pursued in religious humility, in a spirit proper to the subject in hand. And there was much opportunity for study. Bill Bull did not easily yield; night after night he continued to shift from heroic resistance to terror and back to heroic resistance again. All this time Terry Lute sat watching. He gave no heed whatsoever to the words of Parson Down, with which, indeed, he had no concern. He heard nothing; he kept watch—close watch to remember. He opened his heart to the terror of poor Bill Bull; he sought to feel, though the effort was not conscious, what the atheist endured in the presence of the wrath to come. He watched; he memorized every phrase of the torture, as it expressed itself in the changing lines of Bill Bull's countenance, that he might himself express it.

Afterward, in the kitchen, he drew pictures. He drew many; he succeeded in none. He worked in a fever, he destroyed in despair, he began anew with his teeth clenched. And then all at once, a windy night, he gave it all up and came wistfully to sit by the kitchen fire.

"Is you quit?" his mother inquired.

"Ay, Mother."

"H-m-m!" says Skipper Tom, puzzled. "I never knowed you t' quit for the night afore I made you."

Terry Lute shot his father a reproachful glance.

"I must take heed t' my soul," said he, darkly, "lest I be damned for my sins."

Next night Terry Lute knelt at the penitent bench with old Bill Bull. It will be recalled now that he had heard never a word of Parson Down's denunciations and appeals, that he had been otherwise and deeply engaged. His response had been altogether a reflection of Bill Bull's feeling, which he had observed, received, and memorized, and so possessed in the end that he had been overmastered by it, though he was ignorant of what had inspired it. And this, Cobden says, is a sufficient indication of that mastery of subject, of understanding and sympathy, which young Terry Lute later developed and commanded as a great master should, at least to the completion of his picture, in the last example of his work, "The Fang."

At any rate, it must be added that after his conversion Terry Lute was a very good boy for a time.

Terry Lute was in his fourteenth year when he worked on "The Fang." Skipper Tom did not observe the damnable disintegration that occurred, nor was Terry Lute himself at all aware of it. But the process went on, and the issue, a sudden disclosure when it came, was inevitable in the case of Terry Lute. When the northeasterly gales came down with fog, Terry Lute sat on the slimy, wave-lapped ledge overhanging the swirl of water, and watched the spent breaker, streaked with current and flecked with fragments; and he watched, too, the cowering ledge beyond, and the great wave from the sea's restlessness as it thundered into froth and swept on, and the cliff in the mist, and the approach of the offshore ice, and the woeful departure of the last light of day. But he took no pencil to the ledge; he memorized in his way. He kept watch; he brooded.

In this way he came to know in deeper truth the menace of the sea; not to perceive and grasp it fleetingly, not to hold it for the uses of the moment, but surely to possess it in his understanding.

His purpose, avowed with a chuckle, was to convey fear to the beholder of his work. It was an impish trick, and it brought him unwittingly into peril of his soul.

"I 'low," says he between his teeth to Skipper Tom, "that she'll scare the wits out o' *you,* father."

Skipper Tom laughed.

"She'll have trouble," he scoffed, "when the sea herself has failed."

"You jus' wait easy," Terry grimly promised him, "till I gets her off the stocks."

At first Terry Lute tentatively sketched. Bits of the whole were accomplished,—flecks of foam and the lines of a current,—and torn up. This was laborious. Here was toil, indeed, and Terry Lute bitterly complained of it. 'Twas bother; 'twas labor; there wasn't no *sense* to it. Terry Lute's temper went overboard. He sighed and shifted, pouted and whimpered while he worked; but he kept on, with courage equal to his impulse, toiling every evening of that summer until his impatient mother shooed him off to more laborious toil upon the task in his nightmares. The whole arrangement was not attempted for the first time until midsummer. It proceeded, it halted, it vanished. Seventeen efforts were destroyed, ruthlessly thrust into the kitchen stove with no other comment than a sigh, a sniff of disgust, and a shuddering little whimper.

It was a windy night in the early fall of the year, blowing high and wet, when Terry Lute dropped his crayon with the air of not wanting to take it up again.

He sighed, he yawned.

"I got her done," says he, "confound her!" He yawned again.

"Too much labor, lad," Skipper Tom complained.

"Pshaw!" says Terry, indignantly. "I didn't *labor* on her."

Skipper Tom stared aghast in the presence of this monstrously futile prevarication.

"Ecod!" he gasped.

"Why, father," says Terry, airily, "I jus'—sketched her. Do she scare you?"

From Terry Lute's picture Skipper Tom's glance ran to Terry Lute's anxious eyes.

"She do," said he, gravely; "but I'm fair unable t' fathom"—pulling his beard in bewilderment—"the use of it all."

Terry Lute grinned.

It did not appear until the fall gales were blowing in earnest that "The Fang" had made a coward of Terry Lute. There was a gray sea that day, and day was on the wing. There was reeling, noisy water roundabout, turning black in the failing light, and a roaring lee shore; and a gale in the making and a saucy wind were already jumping down from the northeast with a trail of disquieting fog. Terry Lute's spirit failed; he besought, he wept, to be taken ashore. "Oh, I'm woeful scared o' the sea!" he complained. Skipper Tom brought him in from the sea, a whimpering coward, cowering degraded and shamefaced in the stern-sheets of the punt. There were no reproaches. Skipper Tom pulled grimly into harbor. His world had been shaken to ruins; he was grave without hope, as many a man before him has fallen upon the disclosure of inadequacy in his own son.

It was late that night when Skipper Tom and the discredited boy were left alone by the kitchen fire. The gale was down then, a wet wind blowing wildly in from the sea. Tom Lute's cottage shook in its passing fingers, which seemed somehow not to linger long enough to clutch it well, but to grasp in driven haste and sweep on. The boy sat snuggled to the fire for its consolation; he was covered with shame, oppressed, sore, and hopeless. He was disgraced: he was outcast, and now forever, from a world of manly endeavor wherein good courage did the work of the day that every man must do. Skipper Tom, in his slow survey of this aching and pitiful degradation, had an overwhelming sense of fatherhood. He must be wise, he thought; he must be wise and very wary that fatherly helpfulness might work a cure.

The boy had failed, and his failure had not been a thing of unfortuitous chance, not an incident of catastrophe, but a significant expression of character. Terry Lute was a coward, deep down, through and through: he had not lapsed in a panic; he had disclosed an abiding fear of the sea. He was not a coward by any act; no mere wanton folly had disgraced him, but the fallen nature of his own heart. He had failed; but he was only a lad, after all, and he must be helped to overcome. And there he sat, snuggled close to the fire, sobbing now, his face in his hands. Terry Lute knew—that which Skipper Tom did not yet know—that he had nurtured fear of the sea for the scandalous delight of imposing it upon others in the exercise of a devilish impulse and facility.

And he was all the more ashamed. He had been overtaken in iniquity; he was foredone.

"Terry, lad," said Skipper Tom, gently, "you've done ill the day."

"Ay, sir."

"I 'low," Skipper Tom apologized, "that you isn't very well."

"I'm not ailin', sir," Terry whimpered.

"An I was you," Skipper Tom admonished, "I'd not spend time in weepin'."

"I'm woebegone, sir."

"You're a coward, God help you!" Skipper Tom groaned.

"Ay, sir."

Skipper Tom put a hand on the boy's knee. His voice was very gentle.

"There's no place in the world for a man that's afeard o' the sea," he said. "There's no work in the world for a coward t' do. What's fetched you to a pass like this, lad?"

"Broodin', sir."

"Broodin', Terry? What's that?"

"Jus' broodin'."

"Not that damned picture, Terry?"

"Ay, sir."

"How can that be, lad?" It was all incompre-

"'You're a coward, God help you!' Skipper Tom groaned."

hensible to Skipper Tom. "'Tis but an unreal thing."

Terry looked up.

"'Tis *real!*" he blazed.

"'Tis but a thing o' fancy."

"Ay, fancy! A thing o' fancy! 'Tis fancy that *makes* it real."

"An' you—a coward?"

Terry sighed.

"Ay, sir," said he, ashamed.

"Terry Lute," said Skipper Tom, gravely, now perceiving, "is you been fosterin' any fear o' the sea?"

"Ay, sir."

Skipper Tom's eye flashed in horrified understanding. He rose in contempt and wrath.

"*Practicin'* fear o' the sea?" he demanded.

"Ay, sir."

"T' sketch a picture?"

Terry began to sob.

"There wasn't no other way," he wailed.

"God forgive you, wicked lad!"

"I'll overcome, sir."

"Ah, Terry, poor lad," cried Skipper Tom, anguished, "you've no place no more in a decent world."

"I'll overcome."

"'Tis past the time."

Terry Lute caught his father about the neck.

"I'll overcome, father," he sobbed. "I'll overcome."

And Tom Lute took the lad in his arms, as though he were just a little fellow.

And, well, in great faith and affection they made an end of it all that night—a chuckling end, accomplished in the kitchen stove, of everything that Terry Lute had done, saving only "The Fang," which must be kept ever-present, said Skipper Tom, to warn the soul of Terry Lute from the reefs of evil practices. And after that, and through the years since then, Terry Lute labored to fashion a man of himself after the standards of his world. Trouble? Ay, trouble—trouble enough at first, day by day, in fear, to confront the fabulous perils of his imagination. Trouble enough thereafter encountering the sea's real assault, to subdue the reasonable terrors of those parts. Trouble enough, too, by and by, to devise perils beyond the common, to find a madcap way, to disclose a chance worth daring for the sheer exercise of courage. But from all these perils, of the real and the fanciful, of the commonplace path and the way of reckless ingenuity, Terry Lute emerged at last with the reputation of having airily outdared every devil of the waters of Out-of-the-Way.

When James Cobden came wandering by, Terry Lute was a great, grave boy, upstanding, sure-eyed, unafraid, lean with the labor he had done upon his own soul.

When the *Stand By,* in from Twillingate Harbor, dropped anchor at Out-of-the-Way Tickle, James Cobden had for three days lived intimately with "The Fang." He was hardly to be moved from its company. He had sought cause of offense; he had found no reasonable grounds. Wonder had grown within him. Perhaps from this young work he had visioned the highest fruition of the years. The first warm flush of approbation, at any rate, had changed to the beginnings of reverence. That Terry Lute was a master—a master of magnitude, already, and of a promise so large that in generations the world had not known the like of it—James Cobden was gravely persuaded. And this meant much to James Cobden, clear, aspiring soul, a man in pure love with his art. And there was more: grown old now, a little, he dreamed new dreams of fatherly affection, indulged in a studio which had grown lonely of late; and he promised himself, beyond this, the fine delight of cherishing a young genius, himself the prophet of that power, with whose great fame his own name might bear company into the future. And Terry Lute, met in the flesh, turned out to be a man—even such a man, in his sure, wistful strength, as Cobden could respect.

There came presently the close of a day on the cliffs of Out-of-the-Way, a blue wind blowing over the sunlit moss, when Cobden, in fear of the issue, which must be challenged at last, turned from his work to the slope behind, where Terry Lute sat watching.

"Come!" said Cobden, smiling, "have a try."

Terry Lute shrank amused from the extended color-box and brushes.

"Ah, no, sir," said he, blushing. "I used t', though, when I were a child."

Cobden blinked.

"Eh?" he ejaculated.

"I isn't done nothin' at it since."

" 'I put away childish things,' " flashed inevitably into Cobden's mind. He was somewhat alarmed. "Why not since then?" he asked.

" 'Tis not a man's work, sir."

"Again, why not?"

" 'Tis a sort o'—silly thing—t' do."

"Good God!" Cobden thought, appalled. "The lad has strangled his gift!"

Terry Lute laughed then.

"I'm sorry, sir," he said quickly, with a wistful smile, seeking forgiveness; "but I been watchin' you workin' away there like mad with all them little brushes. An' you looked so sort o' funny, sir, that I jus' couldn't help—laughin'." Again he threw back his head, and once more, beyond his will, and innocent of offense and blame, he laughed a great, free laugh.

It almost killed James Cobden.

IV

THE DOCTOR OF AFTERNOON ARM

IV

THE DOCTOR OF AFTERNOON ARM

IT was March weather. There was sunshine and thaw. Anxious Bight was caught over with rotten ice from Ragged Run Harbor to the heads of Afternoon Arm. A rumor of seals on the Arctic drift ice off shore had come in from the Spotted Horses. It inspired instant haste in all the cottages of Ragged Run—an eager, stumbling haste. In Bad-Weather Tom West's kitchen, somewhat after ten o'clock in the morning, in the midst of this hilarious scramble to be off to the floe, there was a flash and spit of fire, and the clap of an explosion, and the clatter of a sealing-gun on the bare floor; and in the breathless, dead little interval between the appalling detonation and a man's groan of dismay followed by a woman's choke and scream of terror, Dolly West, Bad-Weather Tom's small maid, stood swaying, wreathed in gray smoke, her little hands pressed tight to her eyes.

She was—or rather had been—a pretty little creature. There had been yellow curls—in the Newfoundland way—and rosy cheeks and grave blue eyes; but now of all this shy, fair loveliness——

"You've killed her!"

"No—no!"

Dolly dropped her hands. She reached out, then, for something to grasp. And she plainted: "I ithn't dead, mother. I juth—I juth can't thee." She extended her hands. They were discolored, and there was a slow, red drip. "They're all wet!" she complained.

By this time the mother had the little girl gathered close in her arms. She moaned: "The doctor!"

Terry West caught up his cap and mittens and sprang to the door.

"Not by the Bight!" Bad-Weather shouted.

"No, sir."

Dolly West whimpered: "It thmart-th, mother!"

"By Mad Harry an' Thank-the-Lord!"

"Ay, sir."

Dolly screamed—now: "It hurt-th! Oh, oh, it hurt-th!"

"An' haste, lad!"

"Ay, sir."

There was no doctor in Ragged Run Harbor; there was a doctor at Afternoon Arm, however—across Anxious Bight. Terry West avoided the rotten ice of the Bight and took the 'longshore trail by way of Mad Harry and Thank-the-Lord. At noon he was past Mad Harry, his little legs wearing well and his breath coming easily through his expanded nostrils. He had not paused; and at four o'clock—still on a dogtrot—he had hauled down the chimney smoke of Thank-the-Lord and was bearing up for Afternoon Arm.

Early dusk caught him shortcutting the doubtful ice of Thank-the-Lord Cove; and half an hour later, midway of the passage to Afternoon Arm, with two miles left to accomplish—dusk falling thick and cold, then, a frosty wind blowing—Creep Head of the Arm looming black and solid—he dropped through the ice and vanished.

Returning from a professional call at Tumble Tickle in clean, sunlit weather, with nothing more tedious than eighteen miles of wilderness trail and rough floe ice behind him, Doctor Rolfe was chagrined to discover himself fagged out. He had come heartily down the trail from Tumble Tickle, but on the ice in the shank of the day—there had been eleven miles of the floe—he had lagged and complained under what was indubitably the weight of his sixty-three years. He was slightly perturbed. He had been fagged out before, to be sure. A man cannot practice medicine out of a Newfoundland outport harbor for thirty-seven years and not know what it means to stomach a physical exhaustion. It was not that. What perturbed Doctor Rolfe was the singular coincidence of a touch of melancholy with the ominous complaint of his lean old legs.

And presently there was a more disquieting revelation. In the drear, frosty dusk, when he rounded Creep Head, opened the lights of Afternoon Arm, and caught the warm, yellow gleam of the lamp in the surgery window, his expectation ran all at once to his supper and his bed. He was hungry—that was true. Sleepy? No; he was not sleepy. Yet he wanted to go to bed. Why? He wanted to go to bed in the way that old men want to go to bed—less to sleep than just to sigh and stretch out and rest. And this anxious wish for bed—just to stretch out and rest—held its definite implication. It was more than symptomatic—it was shocking.

"That's age!"

It was.

"Hereafter, as an old man should," Doctor Rolfe resolved, "I go with caution and I take my ease."

And it was in this determination that Doctor Rolfe opened the surgery door and came gratefully into the warmth and light and familiar odors of the little room. Caution was the wisdom and privilege of age, wasn't it? he reflected after supper in the glow of the surgery fire. There was no shame in it, was there? Did duty require of a man that he should practice medicine out of Afternoon Arm for thirty-seven years—in all sorts of weather and along a hundred and thirty miles of the worst coast in the world—and go recklessly into a future of increasing inadequacy? It did not! He had stood his watch. What did he owe life? Nothing—nothing! He had paid in full. Well, then, what did life owe him? It owed him something, didn't it? Didn't life owe him at least an old age of reasonable ease and self-respecting independence? It did!

By this time the more he reflected, warming his lean, aching shanks the while, the more he dwelt upon the bitter incidents of that one hundred and thirty miles of harsh coast, through the thirty-seven years he had managed to survive the winds and seas and frosts of it; and the more he dwelt upon his straitened circumstances and increasing age the more petulant he grew.

It was in such moods as this that Doctor Rolfe was accustomed to recall the professional services he had rendered and to dispatch bills therefor; and now he fumbled through the litter of his old desk for pen and ink, drew a dusty, yellowing sheaf of statements of accounts from a dusty pigeonhole, and set himself to work, fuming and grumbling all the while. "I'll tilt the fee!" he determined. This was to be the new policy—to "tilt the fee," to demand payment, to go with caution; in this way to provide for an old age of reasonable ease and self-respecting independence. And Doctor Rolfe began to make out statements of accounts due for services rendered.

From this labor and petulant reflection Doctor Rolfe was withdrawn by a tap on the surgery door. He called "Come in!" with no heart for the event. It was no night to be abroad on the ice. Yet the tap could mean but one thing—somebody was in trouble; and as he called "Come in!" and looked up from the statement of account, and while he waited for the door to open, his pen poised and his face in a pucker of trouble, he considered the night and wondered what strength was left in his lean old legs.

A youngster—he had been dripping wet and was now sparkling all over with frost and ice—intruded.

"Thank-the-Lord Cove?"

"No, sir."

"Mad Harry?"

"Ragged Run, sir."

"Bad-Weather West's lad?"

"Yes, sir."

"Been in the water?"

The boy grinned. He was ashamed of himself. "Yes, sir. I falled through the ice, sir."

"Come across the Bight?"

The boy stared. "No, sir. A cat couldn't cross the Bight the night, sir. 'Tis all rotten. I come alongshore by Mad Harry an' Thank-the-Lord. I dropped through all of a sudden, sir, in Thank-the-Lord Cove."

"Who's sick?"

"Pop's gun went off, sir."

Doctor Rolfe rose. " 'Pop's gun went off!' Who was in the way?"

"Dolly, sir."

"And Dolly in the way! And Dolly——"

"She've gone blind, sir. An' her cheek, sir—an' one ear, sir——"

"What's the night?"

"Blowin' up, sir. There's a scud. An' the moon——"

"You didn't cross the Bight? Why not?"

"'Tis rotten from shore t' shore. I'd not try the Bight, sir, the night."

"No?"

"No, sir." The boy was very grave.

"Mm-m."

All this while Doctor Rolfe had been moving about the surgery in sure haste—packing a waterproof case with little instruments and vials and what not. And now he got quickly into his boots and jacket, pulled down his coonskin cap, pulled up his sealskin gloves, handed Bad-Weather West's boy over to his housekeeper for supper and bed (he was a bachelor man), and closed the surgery door upon himself.

Doctor Rolfe took to the harbor ice and drove head down into the gale. There were ten miles to go. It was to be a night's work. He settled himself doggedly. It was heroic. In the circumstances, however, this aspect of the night's work was not stimulating to a tired old man. It was a mile and a half to Creek Head, where Afternoon Tickle led a narrow way from the shelter of Afternoon Arm to Anxious Bight and the open sea; and from the lee of Creep Head—a straightaway across Anxious Bight—it was nine miles to Blow-me-

Down Dick of Ragged Run Harbor. And Doctor Rolfe had rested but three hours. And he was old.

Impatient to revive the accustomed comfort and glow of strength he began to run. When he came to Creep Head and there paused to survey Anxious Bight in a flash of the moon, he was tingling and warm and limber and eager. Yet he was dismayed by the prospect. No man could cross from Creep Head to Blow-me-Down Dick of Ragged Run Harbor in the dark. Doctor Rolfe considered the light. Communicating masses of ragged cloud were driving low across Anxious Bight. Offshore there was a sluggish bank of black cloud. The moon was risen and full. It was obscured. The intervals of light were less than the intervals of shadow. Sometimes a wide, impenetrable cloud, its edges alight, darkened the moon altogether. Still, there was light enough. All that was definitely ominous was the bank of black cloud lying sluggishly offshore. The longer Doctor Rolfe contemplated its potentiality for catastrophe the more he feared it.

"If I were to be overtaken by snow!"

It was blowing high. There was the bite and shiver of frost in the wind. Half a gale ran in from the open sea. Midway of Anxious Bight it would be a saucy, hampering, stinging head wind. And beyond Creep Head the ice was in doubtful condition. A man might conjecture; that was all. It was mid-spring. Freezing weather had of late alternated with periods of thaw and rain. There had been windy days. Anxious Bight had even once been clear of ice. A westerly wind had broken the ice and swept it out beyond the heads. In a gale from the northeast, however, these fragments had returned with accumulations of Arctic pans and hummocks from the Labrador current; and a frosty night had caught them together and sealed them to the cliffs of the coast. It was a most delicate attachment—one pan to the other and the whole to the rocks. It had yielded somewhat—it must have gone rotten—in the weather of that day. What the frost had accomplished since dusk could be determined only upon trial.

"Soft as cheese!" Doctor Rolfe concluded. "Rubber ice and air holes!"

There was another way to Ragged Run—the way by which Terry West had come. It skirted the shore of Anxious Bight—Mad Harry and Thank-the-Lord and Little Harbor Deep—and something more than multiplied the distance by one and a half. Doctor Rolfe was completely aware of the difficulties of Anxious Bight—the way from Afternoon Arm to Ragged Run; the treacherous reaches of young ice, bending under the weight of a man; the veiled black water; the labor, the crevices, the snow crust of the Arctic pans and hummocks; and the broken field and wash of the sea beyond the lesser island of the Spotted Horses. And he knew, too, the issue of the disappearance of the moon, the desperate plight into which the sluggish bank of black cloud might plunge a man. As a matter of unromantic fact he desired greatly to decline a passage of Anxious Bight that night.

Instead he moved out and shaped a course for the black bulk of the Spotted Horses. This was in the direction of Blow-me-Down Dick of Ragged Run, and the open sea.

He sighed. "If I had a son——" he reflected.

Well, now, Doctor Rolfe was a Newfoundlander. He was used to traveling all sorts of ice in all sorts of weather. The returning fragments of the ice of Anxious Bight had been close packed for two miles beyond the narrows of Afternoon Arm by the northeast gale which had driven them back from the open. This was rough ice. In the press of the wind the drifting floe had buckled. It had been a big gale. Under the whip of it the ice had come down with a rush. And when it encountered the coast the first great pans had been thrust out of the sea by the weight of the floe behind. A slow pressure had even driven them up the cliffs of Creep Head and heaped them in a tumble below. It was thus a folded, crumpled floe, a vast field of broken bergs and pans at angles.

No Newfoundlander would adventure on the ice without a gaff. A gaff is a lithe, ironshod pole, eight or ten feet in length. Doctor Rolfe was as cunning and sure with a gaff as any old hand of the sealing fleet. He employed it now to advantage. It was a vaulting pole. He walked less than he leaped. This was no work for the half light of an obscured moon. Sometimes he halted for light; but delay annoyed him. A pause of ten minutes—he squatted for rest meantime—threw him into a state of incautious irritability. At this rate it would be past dawn before he made the cottages of Ragged Run Harbor.

Impatient of precaution, he presently chanced a leap. It was error. As the meager light disclosed the path a chasm of fifteen feet intervened between the edge of the upturned pan upon which he stood and a flat-topped hummock of Arctic ice to which he was bound. There was footing for the tip of his gaff midway below. He felt for this footing to entertain himself while the moon delayed. It was there. He was tempted. The chasm was critically deep for the length of the gaff. Worse than that, the hummock was higher than the pan. Doctor Rolfe peered across. It was not *much* higher. It would merely be necessary to lift stoutly at the climax of the leap. And there was need of haste—a little maid in hard case at Ragged Run and a rising cloud threatening black weather.

A slow cloud covered the moon. It was aggravating. There would be no light for a long time. A man must take a chance——. And all at once the old man gave way to impatience; he gripped his gaff with angry determination and projected himself toward the hummock of Arctic ice. A flash later he had regretted the hazard. He perceived that he had misjudged the height of the hummock. Had the gaff been a foot longer he would have cleared the chasm. It occurred to him that he would break his back and merit the fate of his callow mistake. Then his toes caught the edge of the flat-topped hummock. His boots were of soft seal leather. He gripped the ice. And now he hung suspended and inert. The slender gaff bent under the prolonged strain of his weight and shook in response to a shiver of his arms. Courage failed a little. Doctor Rolfe was an old man. And he was tired. And he felt unequal——

Dolly West's mother—with Dolly in her arms, resting against her soft, ample bosom—sat by the kitchen fire. It was long after dark. The wind was up; the cottage shook in the squalls. She had long ago washed Dolly's eyes and temporarily stanched the terrifying flow of blood; and now she waited, rocking gently and sometimes crooning a plaintive song of the coast to the restless child.

Tom West came in.

"Hush!"

"Is she sleepin' still?"

"Off an' on. She's in a deal o' pain. She cries out, poor lamb!" Dolly stirred and whimpered. "Any sign of un, Tom?"

"If he comes by the bight he'll never get here at all."

"'Tis not time."

"He might——"

"'Twill be hours afore he comes. I'm jus' wonderin'——"

"Hush!" Dolly moaned. "Ay, Tom?"

"Terry's but a wee feller. I'm wonderin' if he——"

The woman was confident. "He'll make it," she whispered.

"Ay; but if he's delayed——"

"He was there afore dusk. An' the doctor got underway across the Bight——"

"He'll not come by the Bight!"

"He'll come by the Bight. I knows that man. He'll come by the Bight—an' he'll——"

"If he comes by the Bight he'll never get here at all. The Bight's breakin' up. There's rotten ice beyond the Spotted Horses. An' Tickle-my-Ribs is——"

"He'll come. He'll be here afore——"

"There's a gale o' snow comin' down. 'Twill cloud the moon. A man would lose hisself——"

"He'll come."

Bad-Weather Tom West went out again—to plod once more down the narrows to the base of Blow-me-Down Dick and search the vague light of the coast for the first sight of Doctor Rolfe. It was not time; he knew that. There would be hours of waiting. It would be dawn before a man could come by Thank-the-Lord and Mad Harry, if he left

Afternoon Arm even so early as dusk. And as for crossing the Bight—no man could cross the Bight. It was blowing up too—clouds rising and a threat of snow abroad. Bad-weather Tom glanced apprehensively toward the northeast. It would snow before dawn. The moon was doomed. A dark night would fall. And the Bight—Doctor Rolfe would never attempt to cross the Bight——

Hanging between the hummock and the pan, the gaff shivering under his weight, Doctor Rolfe slowly subsided toward the hummock. A toe slipped. He paused. It was a grim business. The other foot held. The leg, too, was equal to the strain. He wriggled his toe back to its grip on the edge of the ice. It was an improved foothold. He turned then and began to lift and thrust himself backward. A last thrust on the gaff set him on his haunches on the Arctic hummock, and he thanked Providence and went on. And on—and on! There was a deal of slippery crawling to do, of slow, ticklish climbing. Doctor Rolfe rounded bergs, scaled perilous inclines, leaped crevices.

It was cold as death now. Was it ten below? The gale bit like twenty below.

When the big northeast wind drove the ice back into Anxious Bight and heaped it inshore, the pressure had decreased as the mass of the floe diminished in the direction of the sea. The outermost areas had not felt the impact. They had not folded—

had not "raftered." When the wind failed they had subsided toward the open. As they say on the coast, the ice had "gone abroad." It was distributed. And after that the sea had fallen flat; and a vicious frost had caught the floe—widespread now—and frozen it fast. It was six miles from the edge of the raftered ice to the first island of the Spotted Horses. The flat pans were solid enough, safe and easy going; but this new, connecting ice—the lanes and reaches of it——

Doctor Rolfe's succinct characterization of the condition of Anxious Bight was also keen: "Soft as cheese!"

All that day the sun had fallen hot on the young ice in which the scattered pans of the floe were frozen. Some of the wider patches of green ice had been weakened to the breaking point. Here and there they must have been eaten clear through. Doctor Rolfe contemplated an advance with distaste. And by and by the first brief barrier of new ice confronted him. He must cross it. A black film—the color of water in that light—bridged the way from one pan to another. He would not touch it. He leaped it easily. A few fathoms forward a second space halted him. Must he put foot on it? With a running start he could—— Well, he chose not to touch the second space, but to leap it.

Soon a third interval stopped him. No man could leap it. He cast about for another way. There was none. He must run across. He scowled.

Disinclination increased. He snarled: "Green ice!" He crossed then like a cat—on tiptoe and swiftly; and he came to the other side with his heart in a flutter. "Whew!"

The ice had yielded without breaking. It had creaked, perhaps; nothing worse. It was what is called "rubber ice." There was more of it; there were miles of it. The nearer the open sea the more widespread was the floe. Beyond—hauling down the Spotted Horses, which lay in the open—the proportion of new ice would be vastly greater. At a trot for the time over the pans, which were flat, and in delicate, mincing little spurts across the bending ice, Doctor Rolfe proceeded. In a confidence that was somewhat flushed—he had rested—he went forward.

And presently, midway of a lane of green ice, he heard a gurgle as the ice bent under his weight. Water washed his boots. He had been on the lookout for holes. This hole he heard—the spurt and gurgle of it. He had not seen it. Safe across, Doctor Rolfe grinned. It was a reaction of relief. "Whew! *Whew!*" he whistled.

By and by he caught ear of the sea breaking under the wind beyond the Little Spotted Horse. He was nearing the limits of the ice. In full moonlight the whitecaps flashed news of a tumultuous open. A rumble and splash of breakers came down with the gale from the point of the island. It indicated that the sea was working in the passage between the Spotted Horses and Blow-me-down Dick of the Ragged Run coast. The waves would run under the ice, would lift it and break it. In this way the sea would eat its way through the passage. It would destroy the young ice. It would break the pans to pieces and rub them to slush.

Doctor Rolfe must make the Little Spotted Horse and cross the passage between the island and the Ragged Run coast. Whatever the issue of haste, he must carry on and make the best of a bad job. Otherwise he would come to Tickle-my-Ribs, between the Little Spotted Horse and Blow-me-Down Dick of Ragged Run, and be marooned from the main shore. And there was another reason: it was immediate and desperately urgent. As the sea was biting off the ice in Tickle-my-Ribs, so, too, it was encroaching upon the body of the ice in Anxious Bight. Anxious Bight was breaking up. Acres of ice were wrenched from the field at a time and then broken up by the sea. What was the direction of this swift melting? It might take any direction. And a survey of the sky troubled Doctor Rolfe. All this while the light had diminished. It was failing still. It was failing faster. There was less of the moon. By and by it would be wholly obscured.

A man would surely lose his life on the ice in thick weather—on one or other of the reaches of new ice. And thereabouts the areas of young ice were wider. To tiptoe across the yielding film of these dimly visible stretches was instantly and dreadfully dangerous. It was horrifying. A man took his life in his hand every time he left a pan. Doctor Rolfe was not insensitive. He began to sweat—not with labor but with fear. When the ice bent under him he gasped and held his breath; and he came each time to the solid refuge of a pan with his teeth set, his face contorted, his hands clenched—a shiver in the small of his back.

To achieve safety once, however, was not to win a final relief; it was merely to confront, in the same circumstances, a precisely similar peril. Doctor Rolfe was not physically exhausted; every muscle that he had was warm and alert. Yet he was weak; a repetition of suspense had unnerved him. A full hour of this, and sometimes he chattered and shook in a nervous chill. In the meantime he had approached the rocks of the Little Spotted Horse.

In the lee of the Little Spotted Horse the ice had gathered as in a back current. It was close packed alongshore to the point of the island. Between this solidly frozen press of pans and the dissolving field in Anxious Bight there had been a lane of ruffled open water before the frost fell. It measured perhaps fifty yards. It was now black and still, sheeted with new ice which had been delayed in forming by the ripple of that exposed situation. Doctor Rolfe had encountered nothing as doubtful. He paused on the brink. A long, thin line of solid pan ice, ghostly white in the dusk beyond, was attached to the rocks of the Little Spotted Horse. It led all the way to Tickle-my-Ribs. Doctor Rolfe must make that line of solid ice. He must cross the wide lane of black, delicately frozen new ice that lay between and barred his way.

He waited for the moon. When the light broke —a thin, transient gleam—he started. A few fathoms forth the ice began to yield. A moment later he stopped short and recoiled. There was a hole—gaping wide and almost under his feet. He stopped. The water overflowed and the ice cracked. He must not stand still. To avoid a second hole he twisted violently to the right and almost plunged into a third opening. It seemed the ice was rotten from shore to shore. And it was a long way across. Doctor Rolfe danced a zigzag toward the pan ice under the cliffs, spurting forward and retreating and swerving. He did not pause; had he paused he would have dropped through. When he was within two fathoms of the pan ice a foot broke through and tripped him flat on his face. With his weight thus distributed he was momentarily held up. Water squirted and gurgled out of the break—an inch of water, forming a pool. Doctor Rolfe lay still and expectant in this pool.

Dolly West's mother still sat by the kitchen fire. It was long past midnight now.

Once more Bad-Weather Tom tiptoed in from

the frosty night. "Is she sleepin' still?" he whispered.

"Hush! She've jus' toppled off again. She's havin' a deal o' pain, Tom. An' she've been bleedin' again."

"Put her down on the bed, dear."

The woman shook her head. "I'm afeared 'twould start the wounds, Tom. Any sign of un yet, Tom?"

"Not yet."

"He'll come soon."

"No; 'tis not near time. 'Twill be dawn afore he——"

"Soon, Tom."

"He'll be delayed by snow. The moon's near gone. 'Twill be black dark in half an hour. I felt a flake o' snow as I come in. An' he'll maybe wait at Mad Harry——"

"He's comin 'by the Bight, Tom."

Dolly stirred, cried out, awakened with a start, and lifted her bandaged head a little. She did not open her eyes. "Is that you, doctor, sir?"

"Hush!" the mother whispered. "'Tis not the doctor yet."

"When——"

"He's comin'."

"I'll take a look," said Tom. He went out again and stumbled down the path to Blow-me-Down Dick by Tickle-my-Ribs.

Doctor Rolfe lay still and expectant in the pool of water near the pan ice and rocks of the Little Spotted Horse. He waited. Nothing happened. Presently he ventured delicately to take off a mitten, to extend his hand, to sink his fingernails in the ice and try to draw himself forward. It was a failure. His fingernails were too short. He could merely scratch the ice. He reflected that if he did not concentrate his weight—that if he kept it distributed—he would not break through. And once more he tried to make use of his fingernails. It turned out that the nails of the other hand were longer. Doctor Rolfe managed to gain half an inch before they slipped. They slipped again—and again and again. It was hopeless. Doctor Rolfe lay still, pondering.

Presently he shot his gaff toward the pan ice, to be rid of the incumbrance of it, and lifted himself on his palms and toes. By this the distribution of his weight was not greatly disturbed. It was not concentrated upon one point. It was divided by four and laid upon four points. And there were no fearsome consequences. It was a hopeful experiment.

Doctor Rolfe stepped by inches on his hands toward the pan ice—dragging his toes. In this way he came to the line of solid ice under the cliffs of the Little Spotted Horse and had a clear path forward. Whereupon he picked up his gaff, and set out for the point of the Little Spotted Horse and the passage of Tickle-my-Ribs. He was heartened.

Tickle-my-Ribs was heaving. The sea had by this time eaten its way clear through the passage from the open to the first reaches of Anxious Bight and far and wide beyond. The channel was half a mile long; in width a quarter of a mile at the narrowest. Doctor Rolfe's path was determined. It must lead from the point of the island to the base of Blow-me-Down Dick and the adjoining fixed and solid ice of the narrows to Ragged Run Harbor. Ice choked the channel. It was continuously running in from the open. It was a thin sheet of fragments. There was only an occasional considerable pan. A high sea ran outside. Waves from the open slipped under this field of little pieces and lifted it in running swells. No single block of ice was at rest.

Precisely as a country doctor might petulantly regard a stretch of hub-deep crossroad, Doctor Rolfe, the outport physician, complained of the passage of Tickle-my-Ribs. Not many of the little pans would bear his weight. They would sustain it momentarily. Then they would tip or sink. There would be foothold through the instant required to choose another foothold and leap toward it. Always the leap would have to be taken from sinking ground. When he came, by good chance, to a pan that would bear him up for a moment, Doctor Rolfe would have instantly to discover another heavy block to which to shape his agitated course. There would be no rest, no certainty beyond the impending moment. But, leaping thus, alert and agile and daring, a man might——

Might? Mm-m, a man might! And he might not! There were contingencies: A man might leap short and find black water where he had depended upon a footing of ice; a man might land on the edge of a pan and fall slowly back for sheer lack of power to obtain a balance; a man might misjudge the strength of a pan to bear him up; a man might find no ice near enough for the next immediately imperative leap; a man might be unable either to go forward or retreat. And there was the light to consider. A man might be caught in the dark. He would be in hopeless case if caught in the dark.

Light was imperative. Doctor Rolfe glanced aloft. "Whew!" he whistled.

The moon and the ominous bank of black cloud were very close. There was snow in the air. A thickening flurry ran past.

Bad-Weather Tom West was not on the lookout when Doctor Rolfe opened the kitchen door at Ragged Run Harbor and strode in with the air of a man who had survived difficulties and was proud of it. Bad-weather Tom West was sitting by the fire, his face in his hands; and the mother of Dolly West—with Dolly still restlessly asleep in her arms—was rocking, rocking, as before.

And Doctor Rolfe set to work—in a way so

gentle, with a voice so persuasive, with a hand so tender and sure, with a skill and wisdom so keen, that little Dolly West, who was brave enough in any case, as you know, yielded the additional patience and courage which the simple means at hand for her relief required; and Doctor Rolfe laved Dolly West's blue eyes until she could see again, and sewed up her wounds that night so that no scar remained; and in the broad light of the next day picked out grains of powder until not a single grain was left to disfigure the child.

Three months after that it again occurred to Doctor Rolfe, of Afternoon Arm, that the practice of medicine was amply provided with hardship and shockingly empty of pecuniary reward. Since the night of the passage of Anxious Bight he had not found time to send out any statements of accounts. It occurred to him that he had then determined, after a reasonable and sufficient consideration of the whole matter, to "tilt the fee." Very well; he would "tilt the fee." He would provide for himself an old age of reasonable ease and self-respecting independence.

Thereupon Doctor Rolfe prepared a statement of account for Bad-Weather West, of Ragged Run Harbor, and after he had written the amount of the bill—"$4"—he thoughtfully crossed it out and wrote "$1.75."

V

A CRŒSUS OF GINGERBREAD COVE

V

A CRŒSUS OF GINGERBREAD COVE

MY name's Race. I've traded these here Newfoundland north-coast outports for salt-fish for half a lifetime. Boy and youth afore that I served Pinch-a-Penny Peter in his shop at Gingerbread Cove. I was born in the Cove. I knowed all the tricks of Pinch-a-Penny's trade. And I tells you it was Pinch-a-Penny Peter's conscience that made Pinch-a-Penny rich. That's queer two ways: you wouldn't expect a north-coast trader to have a conscience; and you wouldn't expect a north-coast trader with a conscience to be rich. But conscience is much like the wind: it blows every which way; and if a man does but trim his sails to suit, he can bowl along in any direction without much wear and tear of the spirit. Pinch-a-Penny bowled along, paddle-punt fisherman to Gingerbread merchant. He went where he was bound for, wing-and-wing to the breeze behind, and got there with his peace of mind showing never a sign of the weather. In my day the old codger had an easy conscience and twenty thousand dollars.

Long Tom Lane, of Gingerbread Cove, vowed in

his prime that he'd sure have to even scores with Pinch-a-Penny Peter afore he could pass to his last harbor with any satisfaction.

"With me, Tom?" says Pinch-a-Penny. "That's a saucy notion for a hook-an'-line man."

"Ten more years o' life," says Tom, "an' I'll square scores."

"Afore you evens scores with me, Tom," says Peter, "you'll have t' have what I wants an' can't get."

"There's times," says Tom, "when a man stands in sore need o' what he never thought he'd want."

"When you haves what I needs," says Peter, "I'll pay what you asks."

"If 'tis for sale," says Tom.

"Money talks," says Peter.

"Ah, well," says Tom, "maybe it don't speak my language."

Pinch-a-Penny Peter's conscience was just as busy as any other man's conscience. And it liked its job. It troubled Pinch-a-Penny. It didn't trouble un to be honest; it troubled un to be rich. And it give un no rest. When trade was dull—no fish coming into Pinch-a-Penny's storehouses and no goods going out of Pinch-a-Penny's shop—Pinch-a-Penny's conscience made un grumble and groan like the damned. I never seed a man so tortured by conscience afore nor since. And to ease his conscience Pinch-a-Penny would go over his ledgers by night; and he'd jot down a gallon of molasses here, and a pound of tea there, until he had made a good day's trade of a bad one. 'Twas simple enough, too; for Pinch-a-Penny never gived out no accounts to amount to nothing, but just struck his balances to please his greed at the end of the season, and told his dealers how much they owed him or how little he owed them.

In dull times Pinch-a-Penny's conscience irked him into overhauling his ledgers. 'Twas otherwise in seasons of plenty. But Pinch-a-Penny's conscience kept pricking away just the same—aggravating him into getting richer and richer. No rest for Pinch-a-Penny! He had to have all the money he could take by hook and crook or suffer the tortures of an evil conscience. Just like any other man, Pinch-a-penny must ease that conscience or lose sleep o' nights. And so in seasons of plenty up went the price of tea at Pinch-a-Penny's shop. And up went the price of pork. And up went the price of flour. All sky-high, ecod! Never was such harsh times, says Peter; why, my dear man, up St. John's way, says he, you couldn't touch tea nor pork nor flour with a ten-foot sealing-gaff; and no telling what the world was coming to, with prices soaring like a gull in a gale and all the St. John's merchants chary of credit!

"Damme!" said Pinch-a-Penny; " 'tis awful times for us poor traders. No tellin' who'll weather this here panic. I'd not be surprised if we got a war out of it."

Well, now, on the Newfoundland north-coast in them days 'twasn't much like the big world beyond. Folk didn't cruise about. They was too busy. And they wasn't used to it, anyhow. Gingerbread Cove folk wasn't born at Gingerbread Cove, raised at Rickity Tickle, married at Seldom-Come-By, aged at Skeleton Harbor, and buried at Run-by-Guess; they were born and buried at Gingerbread Cove. So what the fathers thought at Gingerbread Cove the sons thought; and what the sons knowed had been knowed by the old men for a good many years. Nobody was used to changes. They was shy of changes. New ways was fearsome. And so the price of flour was a mystery. It is, anyhow—wherever you finds it. It always has been. And why it should go up and down at Gingerbread Cove was beyond any man of Gingerbread Cove to fathom. When Pinch-a-Penny said the price of flour was up—well, then, she was up; and that's all there was about it. Nobody knowed no better. And Pinch-a-Penny had the flour.

Pinch-a-Penny had the pork, too. And he had the sweetness and the tea. And he had the shoes and the clothes and the patent medicines. And he had the twine and the salt. And he had all the cash there was at Gingerbread Cove. And he had the schooner that fetched in the supplies and carried away the fish to the St. John's markets. He was the only trader at Gingerbread Cove; his storehouses and shop was fair jammed with the things the folk of Gingerbread Cove couldn't do without and wasn't able to get nowhere else. So, all in all, Pinch-a-Penny Peter could make trouble for the folk that made trouble for he. And the folk grumbled. By times, ecod, they grumbled like the devil of a a fine Sunday morning! But 'twas all they had the courage to do. And Pinch-a-Penny let un grumble away. The best cure for grumbling, says he, was to give it free course. If a man could speak out in meeting, says he, he'd work no mischief in secret.

"Sea-lawyers, eh?" says Peter. "Huh! What you fellers want, anyhow? Huh? You got everything now that any man could expect. Isn't you housed? Isn't you fed? Isn't you clothed? Isn't you got a parson and a schoolmaster? Damme, I believes you wants a doctor settled in the harbor! A doctor! An' 'tisn't two years since I got you your schoolmaster! Queer times we're havin' in the outports these days, with every harbor on the coast wantin' a doctor within hail. You're well enough done by at Gingerbread Cove. None better nowhere. An' why? Does you ever think o' that? Why? Because I got my trade here. An' think o' *me!* Damme, if ar a one o' you had my brain-labor t' do, you'd soon find out what harsh labor was like. What with bad debts an' roguery an' failed seasons an' creditors t' St. John's I'm hard put to it t' keep my seven senses. An' small thanks I gets—me that keeps this harbor alive, in famine an' plenty. 'Tis the business I haves that keeps you. You make trouble for my business, ecod, an' you'll come t' starvation! Now, you mark me!"

There would be a scattered time when Pinch-a-Penny would yield an inch. Oh, ay! I've knowed Pinch-a-Penny to drop the price of stick-candy when he had put the price of flour too high for anybody's comfort.

Well, now, Long Tom Lane, of Gingerbread Cove, had a conscience, too. But 'twas a common conscience. Most men haves un. And they're irksome enough for some. 'Twas not like Pinch-a-Penny Peter's conscience. Nothing useful ever come of it. 'Twas like yours and mine. It troubled Tom Lane to be honest and it kept him poor. All Tom Lane's conscience ever aggravated him to do was just to live along in a religious sort of fashion and rear his family and be decently stowed away in the graveyard when his time was up if the sea didn't cotch un first. But 'twas a busy conscience for all that —and as sharp as a fish-prong. No rest for Tom Lane if he didn't fatten his wife and crew of little lads and maids! No peace of mind for Tom if he didn't labor! And so Tom labored and labored and labored. Dawn to dusk his punt was on the grounds off Lack-a-Day Head, taking fish from the sea to be salted and dried and passed into Pinch-a-Penny's storehouses.

When Tom Lane was along about fourteen years

old his father died. 'Twas of a Sunday afternoon that we stowed un away. I mind the time: spring weather and a fair day, with the sun low, and the birds twittering in the alders just afore turning in.

Pinch-a-Penny Peter cotched up with young Tom on the road home from the little graveyard on Sunset Hill.

"Well, lad," says he, "the old skipper's gone."

"Ay, sir, he's dead an' buried."

"A fine man," says Pinch-a-Penny. "None finer."

With that young Tom broke out crying. "He were a kind father t' we," says he. "An' now he's dead!"

"You lacked nothin' in your father's lifetime," says Peter.

"An' now he's dead!"

"Well, well, you've no call t' be afeared o' goin' hungry on that account," says Peter, laying an arm over the lad's shoulder. "No, nor none o' the little crew over t' your house. Take up the fishin' where your father left it off, lad," says he, "an' you'll find small difference. I'll cross out your father's name on the books an' put down your own in its stead."

"I'm fair obliged," says Tom. "That's kind, sir."

"Nothin' like kindness t' ease sorrow," says Pinch-a-Penny. "Your father died in debt, lad."

"Ay, sir?"

"Deep."

"How much, sir?"

"I'm not able t' tell offhand," says Peter. "'Twas deep enough. But never you care. You'll be able t' square it in course o' time. You're young an' hearty. An' I'll not be harsh. Damme, I'm no skinflint!"

"That's kind, sir."

"You—you—*will* square it?"

"I don't know, sir."

"What?" cries Peter. "What! You're not knowin', eh? That's saucy talk. You had them there supplies?"

"I 'low, sir."

"An' you guzzled your share, I'll be bound!"

"Yes, sir."

"An' your mother had her share?"

"Yes, sir."

"An' you're not knowin' whether you'll pay or not! Ecod! What is you? A scoundrel? A dead beat? A rascal? A thief? A jail-bird?"

"No, sir."

"'Tis for the likes o' you that jails was made."

"Oh, no, sir!"

"Doesn't you go t' church? Is that what they learns you there? I'm thinkin' the parson doesn't earn what I pays un. Isn't you got no conscience?"

'Twas too much for young Tom. You sees, Tom Lane *had* a conscience—a conscience as fresh and as young as his years. And Tom had loved his father well. And Tom honored his father's name. And so when he had brooded over Pinch-a-Penny's words for a spell—and when he had maybe laid awake in the night thinking of his father's goodness—he went over to Pinch-a-Penny's office and allowed he'd pay his father's debt. Pinch-a-Penny give un a clap on the back, and says: "You is an honest lad, Tom Lane! I knowed you was. I'm proud t' have your name on my books!"—and that heartened Tom to continue. And after that Tom kept hacking away on his father's debt. In good years Pinch-a-Penny would say: "She's comin' down, Tom. I'll just apply the surplus." And in bad he'd say: "You isn't quite cotched up with your own self this season, b'y. A little less pork this season, Tom, an' you'll square this here little balance afore next. I wisht this whole harbor was as honest as you. No trouble, then," says he, "t' do business in a business-like way."

When Tom got over the hill—fifty and more—his father's debt, with interest, according to Pinch-a-Penny's figures, which Tom had no learning to dispute, was more than it ever had been; and his own was as much as he ever could hope to pay. And by that time Pinch-a-Penny Peter was rich, and Long Tom Lane was gone sour.

In the fall of the year when Tom Lane was fifty-three he went up to St. John's in Pinch-a-Penny Peter's supply-schooner. Nobody knowed why. And Tom made a mystery of it. But go he would. And when the schooner got back 'twas said that

Tom Lane had vanished in the city for a day. Why? Nobody knowed. Where? Nobody could find out. Tom wouldn't tell, nor could the gossips gain a word from his wife. And, after that, Tom was a changed man; he mooned a deal, and he would talk no more of the future, but dwelt upon the shortness of a man's days and the quantity of his sin, and labored like mad, and read the Scriptures by candle-light, and sot more store by going to church and prayer-meeting than ever afore. Labor? Ecod, how that poor man labored through the winter! While there was light! And until he fair dropped in his tracks of sheer weariness! 'Twas back in the forest—hauling fire-wood with the dogs and storing it away back of his little cottage under Lend-a-Hand Hill.

"Dear man!" says Peter; "you've firewood for half a dozen winters."

"They'll need it," says Tom.

"Ay," says Peter; "but will you lie idle next winter?"

"Next winter?" says Tom. And he laughed. "Oh, next winter," says he, "I'll have another occupation."

"Movin' away, Tom?"

"Well," says Tom, "I is an' I isn't."

There come a day in March weather of that year when seals was thick on the floe off Gingerbread Cove. You could see un with the naked eye from Lack-a-Day Head. A hundred thousand black specks swarming over the ice three miles and more to sea! "Swiles! Swiles!" And Gingerbread Cove went mad for slaughter. 'Twas a fair time for off-shore sealing, too—a blue, still day, with the look and feel of settled weather. The ice had come in from the current with a northeasterly gale, a wonderful mixture of Arctic bergs and Labrador pans, all blinding white in the spring sun; and 'twas a field so vast, and jammed so tight against the coast, that there wasn't much more than a lane or two and a Dutchman's breeches of open water within sight from the heads. Nobody looked for a gale of off-shore wind to blow that ice afore dawn of the next day.

"A fine, soft time, lads!" says Pinch-a-Penny. "I 'low I'll go out with the Gingerbread crew."

"Skipper Peter," says Tom Lane, "you're too old a man t' be on the ice."

"Ay," says Peter, "but I wants t' bludgeon another swile afore I dies."

"But you creaks, man!"

"Ah, well," says Peter, "I'll show the lads I'm able t' haul a swile ashore."

"Small hope for such as you on a movin' floe!"

"Last time, Tom," says Peter.

"Last time, true enough," says Tom, "if that ice starts t' sea with a breeze o' wind behind."

"Oh, well, Tom," says Peter, "I'll take my chances. If the wind comes up I'll be as spry as I'm able."

It come on to blow in the afternoon. But 'twas short warning of off-shore weather. A puff of gray wind come down; a saucier gust went by; and then a swirl of galish wind jumped over the pans. At the first sign of wind, Pinch-a-Penny Peter took for home, loping over the ice as fast as his lungs and old legs would take un when pushed, and nobody worried about he any more. He was in such mad haste that the lads laughed behind un as he passed. Most of the Gingerbread crew followed, dragging their swiles; and them that started early come safe to harbor with the fat. But there's nothing will master a man's caution like the lust of slaughter: give a Newfoundlander a club, and show un a swile-pack, and he'll venture far from safety. 'Twas not until a flurry of snow come along of a sudden that the last of the crew dropped what they was at and begun to jump for shore like a pack of jack-rabbits.

With snow in the wind, 'twas every man for himself. And that means no mercy and less help.

By this time the ice had begun to feel the wind. 'Twas restless. And a bad promise: the pans crunched and creaked as they settled more at ease. The ice was going abroad. As the farther fields drifted off to sea, the floe fell loose inshore. Lanes and pools opened up. The cake-ice tipped and went awash under the weight of a man. Rough going, ecod! There was no telling when open water would cut a man off where he stood. And the wind was whipping off-shore, and the snow was like dust in a man's eyes and mouth, and the landmarks of Gingerbread Cove was nothing but shadows in a mist of snow to windward. Nobody knowed where Pinch-a-Penny Peter was. Nobody thought about him. And wherever poor old Pinch-a-Penny was—whether safe ashore or creaking shoreward against the wind on his last legs—he must do for himself. 'Twas no time to succor rich or poor. Every man for himself and the devil take the hindmost.

Bound out, in the morning, Long Tom Lane had fetched his rodney through the lanes. By luck and good conduct he had managed to get the wee boat a fairish way out. He had beached her, there on the floe—a big pan, close by a hummock which he marked with care. And 'twas for Tom Lane's little rodney that the seven last men of Gingerbread Cove was jumping. With her afloat—and the pack loosening in-shore under the wind—they could make harbor well enough afore the gale worked up the water in the lee of the Gingerbread hills. But she was a mean, small boat. There was room for six, with safety—but room for no more; no room for seven. 'Twas a nasty mess, to be sure. You couldn't expect nothing else. But there wasn't no panic. Gingerbread men was accustomed to tight places. And they took this one easy. Them that got there first launched the boat and stepped in. No fight; no fuss.

It just happened to be Eleazer Butt that was left

'Twas Eleazer's ill-luck. And Eleazer was up in years, and had fell behind coming over the ice.

"No room for me?" says he.

'Twas sure death to be left on the ice. The wind begun to taste of frost. And 'twas jumping up. 'Twould carry the floe far and scatter it broadcast.

"See for yourself, lad," says Tom.

"Pshaw!" says Eleazer. "That's too bad!"

"You isn't no sorrier than me, b'y."

Eleazer tweaked his beard. "Dang it!" says he. "I wisht there *was* room. I'm hungry for my supper."

"Let un in," says one of the lads. "'Tis even chances she'll float it out."

"Well," says Eleazer, "I doesn't want t' make no trouble——"

"Come aboard," says Tom. "An' make haste."

"If she makes bad weather," says Eleazer, "I'll get out."

They pushed off from the pan. 'Twas falling dusk, by this time. The wind blowed black. The frost begun to bite. Snow came thick—just as if, ecod, somebody up aloft was shaking the clouds, like bags, in the gale! And the rodney was deep and ticklish; had the ice not kept the water flat in the lanes and pools, either Eleazer would have had to get out, as he promised, or she would have swamped like a cup. As it was, handled like dynamite, she done well enough; and she might have made harbor within the hour had she not been hailed by Pinch-a-Penny Peter from a small pan of ice midway between.

And there the old codger was squatting, his old face pinched and woebegone, his bag o' bones wrapped up in his coonskin coat, his pan near flush with the sea, with little black waves already beginning to wash over it.

A sad sight, believe me! Poor old Pinch-a-Penny, bound out to sea without hope on a wee pan of ice!

"Got any room for me?" says he.

They ranged alongside. "Mercy o' God!" says Tom; "she's too deep as it is."

"Ay," says Peter; "you isn't got room for no more. She'd sink if I put foot in her."

"Us'll come back," says Tom.

"No use, Tom," says Peter. "You knows that well enough. 'Tis no place out here for a Gingerbread punt. Afore you could get t' shore an' back night will be down an' this here gale will be a blizzard. You'd never be able t' find me."

"I 'low not," says Tom.

"Oh, no," says Peter. "No use, b'y."

"Damme, Skipper Peter," says Tom, "I'm sorry!"

"Ay," says Peter; " 'tis a sad death for an ol' man —squattin' out here all alone on the ice an' shiverin' with the cold until he shakes his poor damned soul out."

"Not damned!" cries Tom. "Oh, don't say it!"

"Ah, well!" says Peter; "sittin' here all alone, I been thinkin'."

" 'Tisn't by any man's wish that you're here, poor man!" says Tom.

"Oh, no," says Peter. "No blame t' nobody. My time's come. That's all. But I wisht I had a seat in your rodney, Tom."

And then Tom chuckled.

"What you laughin' at?" says Peter.

"I got a comical idea," says Tom.

"Laughin' at me, Tom?"

"Oh, I'm jus' laughin'."

" 'Tis neither time nor place, Tom," says Peter, "t' laugh at an old man."

Tom roared. Ay, he slapped his knee, and he throwed back his head, and he roared. 'Twas enough almost to swamp the boat.

"For shame!" says Peter. And more than Pinch-a-Penny thought so.

"Skipper Peter," says Tom, "you're rich, isn't you?"

"I got money," says Peter.

"Sittin' out here, all alone," says Tom, "you been thinkin' a deal, you says?"

"Well," says Peter, "I'll not deny that I been havin' a little spurt o' sober thought."

"You been thinkin' that money wasn't much, after all?"

"Ay."

"An' that all your money in a lump wouldn't buy you passage ashore?"

"Oh, some few small thoughts on that order," says Peter. " 'Tis perfectly natural."

"Money talks," says Tom.

"Tauntin' me again, Tom?"

"No, I isn't," says Tom. "I means it. Money talks. What'll you give for my seat in the boat?"

" 'Tis not for sale, Tom."

The lads begun to grumble. It seemed just as if Long Tom Lane was making game of an old man in trouble. 'Twas either that or lunacy. And there was no time for nonsense off the Gingerbread coast in a spring gale of wind.

"Hist!" Tom whispered to the lads. "I knows what I'm doin'."

"A mad thing, Tom!"

"Oh, no!" says Tom. " 'Tis the cleverest thing ever I thought of. Well," says he to Peter, "how much?"

"No man sells his life."

"Life or no life, my place in this boat is for sale," says Tom. "Money talks. Come, now. Speak up. Us can't linger here with night comin' down."

"What's the price, Tom?"

"How much you got, Peter?"

"Ah, well, I can afford a stiffish price, Tom. Anything you say in reason will suit me. You name the price, Tom. I'll pay."

"Ay, ye crab!" says Tom. "I'm namin' prices now. Look out, Peter! You're seventy-three. I'm fifty-three. Will you grant that I'd live t' be as old as you?"

"I'll grant it, Tom."

"I'm not sayin' I would," says Tom. "You mark that."

"Ah, well, I'll grant it, anyhow."

"I been an industrious man all my life, Skipper Peter. None knows it better than you. Will you grant that I'd earn a hundred and fifty dollars a year if I lived?"

"Ay, Tom."

Down come a gust of wind. "Have done!" says one of the lads. "Here's the gale come down with the dark. Us'll all be cast away."

"Rodney's mine, isn't she?" says Tom.

Well, she was. Nobody could say nothing to that. And nobody did.

"That's three thousand dollars, Peter," says Tom. "Three—thousand—dollars!"

"Ay," says Peter, "she calculates that way. But you've forgot t' deduct your livin' from the total. Not that I minds," says he. " 'Tis just a business detail."

"Damme," says Tom. "I'll not be harsh!"

"Another thing, Tom," says Peter. "You're askin' me t' pay for twenty years o' life when I can use but a few. God knows how many!"

"I got you where I wants you," says Tom, "but I isn't got the heart t' grind you. Will you pay two thousand dollars for my seat in the boat?"

"If you is fool enough t' take it, Tom."

"There's something t' boot," says Tom. "I wants t' die out o' debt."

"You does, Tom."

"An' my father's bill is squared?"

"Ay."

"'Tis a bargain!" says Tom. "God witness!"

"Lads," says Pinch-a-Penny to the others in the rodney, "I calls you t' witness that I didn't ask Tom Lane for his seat in the boat. I isn't no coward. I've asked no man t' give up his life for me. This here bargain is a straight business deal. Business is business. 'Tis not my proposition. An' I calls you t' witness that I'm willin' t' pay what he asks. He've something for sale. I wants it. I've the money t' buy it. The price is his. I'll pay it." Then he turned to Tom. "You wants this money paid t' your wife, Tom?"

"Ay," says Tom, "t' Mary. She'll know why."

"Very good," says Pinch-a-Penny. "You've my word that I'll do it. . . . Wind's jumpin' up, Tom."

"I wants your oath. The wind will bide for that. Hold up your right hand."

Pinch-a-Penny shivered in a blast of the gale. "I swears," says he.

"Lads," says Tom, "you'll shame this man to his grave if he fails t' pay!"

"Gettin' dark, Tom," says Peter.

"Ay," says Tom; "'tis growin' wonderful cold

an' dark out here. I knows it well. Put me ashore on the ice, lads."

They landed Tom, then, on a near-by pan. He would have it so.

"Leave me have my way!" says he. "I've done a good stroke o' business."

Presently they took old Pinch-a-Penny aboard in Tom's stead; and just for a minute they hung off Tom's pan to say good-by.

"I sends my love t' Mary an' the children," says he. "You'll not fail t' remember. She'll know why I done this thing. Tell her 'twas a grand chance an' I took it."

"Ay, Tom."

"Fetch in here close," says Tom. "I want's t' talk t' the ol' skinflint you got aboard there. I'll have my say, ecod, at last! Ye crab!" says he, shaking his fist in Pinch-a-Penny's face, when the rodney got alongside. "Ye robber! Ye pinch-a-penny! Ye liar! Ye thief! I done ye! Hear me? I done ye! I vowed I'd even scores with ye afore I died. An' I've done it—I've done it! What did ye buy? Twenty years o' my life! What will ye pay for? Twenty years o' my life!" And he laughed. And then he cut a caper, and come close to the edge of the pan, and shook his fist in Pinch-a-Penny's face again. "Know what I done in St. John's last fall?" says he. "I seen a doctor, ye crab! Know what he told me? No, ye don't! Twenty years o' my life this here ol' skinflint will pay for!" he crowed. "Two thousand dollars he'll put in the hands o' my poor wife!"

Well, well! The rodney was moving away. And a swirl of snow shrouded poor Tom Lane. But they heard un laugh once more.

"My heart is givin' 'way, anyhow!" he yelled. "I didn't have three months t' live!"

Old Pinch-a-Penny Peter done what he said he would do. He laid the money in poor Mary Lane's hands. But a queer thing happened next day. Up went the price of pork at Pinch-a-Penny's shop! And up went the price of tea and molasses! And up went the price of flour!

VI

A MADONNA OF TINKLE TICKLE

VI

A MADONNA OF TINKLE TICKLE

IT was at Soap-an'-Water Harbor, with the trader *Quick as Wink* in from the sudsy seas of those parts, that Tumm, the old clerk, told the singular tale of the Madonna of Tinkle Tickle.

"I'm no hand for sixpenny novels," says he, with a wry glance at the skipper's dog-eared romance. "Nursemaids an' noblemen? I'm chary. I've no love, anyhow, for the things o' mere fancy. But I'm a great reader," he protested, with quick warmth, "o' the tales that are lived under the two eyes in my head. I'm forever in my lib'ry, too. Jus' now," he added, his eye on a dismayed little man from Chain Harbor, "I'm readin' the book o' the cook. An' I'm lookin' for a sad endin', ecod, if he keeps on scorchin' the water!"

The squat little Newfoundland schooner was snug in the lee of False Frenchman and down for the night. A wet time abroad: a black wind in the rigging, and the swish and patter of rain on the deck. But the forecastle bogey was roaring, and the forecastle lamp was bright; and the crew—at ease and dry—sprawled content in the forecastle glow.

"Lyin' here at Soap-an'-Water Harbor, with Tinkle Tickle hard-by," the clerk drawled on, "I been thumbin' over the queer yarn o' Mary Mull. An' I been enjoyin' it, too. An old tale—lived long ago. 'Tis a tale t' my taste. It touches the heart of a woman. An' so, lads—'tis a mystery."

Then the tale that was lived page by page under the two eyes in Tumm's head:

"Tim Mull was fair dogged by the children o' Tinkle Tickle in his bachelor days," the tale ran on. "There was that about un, somehow, in eyes or voice, t' win the love o' kids, dogs, an' grandmothers. 'Leave the kids have their way,' says he. 'I likes t' have un t' come t' me. They're no bother at all. Why, damme,' says he, 'they uplift the soul of a bachelor man like me! I loves un.'

" 'You'll be havin' a crew o' your own, some day,' says Tom Blot, 'an' you'll not be so fond o' the company.'

" 'I'll ship all the Lord sends.'

" 'Ah-ha, b'y!' chuckles Tom, 'He've a wonderful store o' little souls up aloft.'

" 'Then,' says Tim, 'I'll thank Un t' be lavish.'

"Tom Blot was an old, old man, long past his labor, creakin' over the roads o' Harbor with a staff t' help his dry legs, an' much give t' broodin' on the things he'd round out in this life. ' 'Tis rare that He's mean with such gifts,' says he. 'But 'tis queer the way He bestows un. Ecod!' says he, in a temper, 'I've never been able t' fathom his ways, old as I is!'

"'I wants a big crew o' lads an' little maids, Tom,' says Tim Mull. 'Can't be too many for *me* if I'm to enjoy my cruise in this world.'

"'They've wide mouths, lad.'

"'Hut!' says Tim. 'What's a man for? *I'll* stuff their little crops. You mark *me,* b'y!'

"So it went with Tim Mull in his bachelor days: he'd forever a maid on his shoulder or a lad by the hand. He loved un. 'Twas knowed that he loved un. There wasn't a man or maid at Tinkle Tickle that didn't know. 'Twas a thing that was called t' mind whenever the name o' Tim Mull come up. 'Can't be too many kids about for Tim Mull!' An' they loved *him.* They'd wait for un t' come in from the sea at dusk o' fine days; an' on fine Sunday afternoons—sun out an' a blue wind blowin'—they'd troop at his heels over the roads an' hills o' the Tickle. They'd have no festival without un. On the eve o' Guy Fawkes, in the fall o' the year, with the Gunpowder Plot t' celebrate, when 't was

> Remember, remember,
> The Fifth o' November!

't was Tim Mull that must wind the fire-balls, an' sot the bonfires, an' put saleratus on the blisters. An' at Christmastide, when the kids o' Harbor come carolin' up the hill, all in mummers' dress, pipin',—

> God rest you, merry gentlemen;
> Let nothin' you dismay!

't was Tim Mull, in his cottage by Fo'c's'le Head, that had a big blaze, an' a cake, an' a tale, an' a tune on the concertina, for the rowdy crew.

" 'I love un!' says he. 'Can't be too many for *me!*'

"An' everybody knowed it; an' everybody wondered, too, how Tim Mull would skipper his own little crew when he'd shipped un.

"Tim Mull fell in love, by-an'-by, with a dark maid o' the Tickle. By this time his mother was dead, an' he lived all alone in the cottage by Fo'c's'le Head. He had full measure o' the looks an' ways that win women. 'Twas the fashion t' fish for un. An' 'twas a thing that was shameless as fashion. Most o' the maids o' Harbor had cast hooks. Polly Twitter, for one, an' in desperation: a pink an' blue wee parcel o' fluff—an' a trim little craft, withal. But Tim Mull knowed nothin' o' this, at all; he was too stupid, maybe,—an' too decent,—t' read the glances an' blushes an' laughter they flung out for bait.

" 'Twas Mary Low—who'd cast no eyes his way—that overcome un. She loved Tim Mull. No doubt, in the way o' maids, she had cherished her hope; an' it may be she had grieved t' see big Tim Mull, entangled in ribbons an' curls an' the sparkle o' blue eyes, indulge the flirtatious ways o' pretty little Polly Twitter. A tall maid, this Mary—soft an' brown. She'd brown eyes, with black lashes to hide un, an' brown hair, growin' low an' curly; an' her round cheeks was brown, too, flushed with red. She was a maid with sweet ways an' a tender pride; she was slow t' speak an' not much give t' laughter; an' she had the sad habit o' broodin' overmuch in the dusk. But she'd eyes for love, never fear, an' her lips was warm; an' there come a night in spring weather—broad moonlight an' a still world—when Tim Mull give way to his courage.

"'Tumm,' says he, when he come in from his courtin', that night, 'there'll be guns poppin' at Tinkle Tickle come Friday.'

"'A weddin'?' says I.

"'Me an' Mary Low, Tumm. I been overcome at last. 'Twas the moon.'

"'She's ever the friend o' maids,' says I.

"'An' the tinkle of a goat's bell on Lookout. It fell down from the slope t' the shadows where the alders arch over the road by Needle Rock. Jus' when me an' Mary was passin' through, Tumm! You'd never believe such an accident. There's no resistin' brown eyes in spring weather. She's a wonderful woman, lad.'

"'That's queer!' says I.

" 'A wonderful woman,' says he. 'No shallow water there. She's deep. I can't *tell* you how wonderful she is. Sure, I'd have t' play it on the concertina.'

" 'I'll lead the chivari,' says I, 'an' you grant me a favor.'

" 'Done!' says he.

" 'Well, Tim,' says I, 'I'm a born godfather.'

" 'Ecod!' says he. An' he slapped his knee an' chuckled. 'Does you mean it? Tobias Tumm Mull! 'Twill be a very good name for the first o' my little crew. Haw, haw! The thing's as good as managed.'

"So they was wed, hard an' fast; an' the women o' Tinkle Tickle laughed on the sly at pretty Polly Twitter an' condemned her shameless ways."

"In the fall o' that year I went down Barbadoes way in a fish-craft from St. John's. An' from Barbadoes, with youth upon me t' urge adventure, I shipped of a sudden for Spanish ports. 'Twas a matter o' four years afore I clapped eyes on the hills o' Tinkle Tickle again. An' I mind well that when the schooner hauled down ol' Fo'c's'le Head, that day, I was in a fret t' see the godson that Tim Mull had promised me. But there wasn't no godson t' see. There wasn't no child at all.

" 'Well, no, Tumm,' says Tim Mull, 'we hasn't been favored in that particular line. But *I'm* content. All the children o' Harbor is mine,' says he, 'jus' as they used t' be, an' there's no sign o' the supply givin' out. Sure, *I've* no complaint o' my fortune in life.'

"Nor did Mary Mull complain. She thrived, as ever: she was soft an' brown an' flushed with the color o' flowers, as when she was a maid; an' she rippled with smiles, as then, in the best of her moods, like the sea on a sunlit afternoon.

" 'I've Tim,' says she, 'an' with Tim I'm content. Your godson, Tumm, had he deigned to sail in, would have been no match for my Tim in goodness.'

"An' still the children o' Tinkle Tickle trooped after Tim Mull; an' still he'd forever a maid on his shoulder or a wee lad by the hand.

" 'Fair winds, Tumm!' says Tim Mull. 'Me an' Mary is wonderful happy t'gether.'

" 'Isn't a thing we could ask for,' says she.

" 'Well, well!' says I. 'Now, that's *good*, Mary!'

"There come that summer t' Tinkle Tickle she that was once Polly Twitter. An' trouble clung to her skirts. Little vixen, she was! No tellin' how deep a wee woman can bite when she've the mind t' put her teeth in. Nobody at Tinkle Tickle but knowed that the maid had loved Tim Mull too well for her peace o' mind. Mary Mull knowed it well enough. Not Tim, maybe. But none better than Mary. 'Twas no secret, at all: for Polly Twitter had carried on like the bereft when Tim Mull was wed—had cried an' drooped an' gone white an' thin, boastin', all the while, t' draw friendly notice, that her heart was broke for good an' all. 'Twas a year an' more afore she flung up her pretty little head an' married a good man o' Skeleton Bight. An' now here she was, come back again, plump an' dimpled an' roguish as ever she'd been in her life. On a bit of a cruise, says she; but 'twas not on a cruise she'd come—'twas t' flaunt her new baby on the roads o' Tinkle Tickle.

"A wonderful baby, ecod! You'd think it t' hear the women cackle o' the quality o' that child. An' none more than Mary Mull. She kissed Polly Twitter, an' she kissed the baby; an' she vowed—with the sparkle o' joyous truth in her wet brown eyes—that the most bewitchin' baby on the coast, the stoutest baby, the cleverest baby, the sweetest baby, had come straight t' Polly Twitter, as though it wanted the very prettiest mother in all the world, an' knowed jus' what it was about.

"An' Polly kissed Mary. 'You is so *kind,* Mary!' says she. ''Tis jus' *sweet* o' you! How *can* you!'

"'Sweet?' says Mary, puzzled. 'Why, no, Polly. I'm—glad.'

"'Is you, Mary? 'Tis so *odd!* Is you really—*glad?*'

"'Why not?'

"'I don't know, Mary,' says Polly. 'But I—I—I 'lowed, somehow—that you wouldn't be—so *very* glad. An' I'm not sure that I'm grateful—enough.'

"An' the women o' Tinkle Tickle wondered, too, that Mary Mull could kiss Polly Twitter's baby. Polly Twitter with a rosy baby,—a lusty young nipper,—an' a lad, t' boot! An' poor Mary Mull with no child, at all, t' bless Tim Mull's house with! An' Tim Mull a lover o' children, as everybody knowed! The men chuckled a little, an' cast winks about, when Polly Twitter appeared on the roads with the baby; for 'twas a comical thing t' see her air an' her strut an' the flash o' pride in her eyes. But the women kep' their eyes an' ears open—an' waited for what might happen. They was all sure, ecod, that there was a gale comin' down; an' they was women,—an' they knowed the hearts o' women, —an' they was wise, if not kind, in their expectation.

"As for Mary Mull, she give never a sign o' trouble, but kep' right on kissin' Polly Twitter's baby, whenever she met it, which Polly contrived t' be often; an' I doubt that she knowed—until she couldn't help knowin'—that there was pity abroad at Tinkle Tickle for Tim Mull.

"'Twas at the Methodist treat on Bide-a-Bit Point that Polly Twitter managed her mischief. 'Twas a time well-chosen, too. Trust the little minx for that! She was swift t' bite—an' clever t' fix her white little fangs. There was a flock o' women, Mary Mull among un, in gossip by the baskets. An' Polly Twitter was there, too,—an' the baby. Sun under a black sea; then the cold breath o' dusk, with fog in the wind, comin' over the hills.

"'Tim Mull,' says Polly, 'hold the baby.'

"'Me?' says he. 'I'm a butterfingers, Polly.'

"'Come!' says she.

"'No, no, Polly! I'm timid.'

"She laughed at that. 'I'd like t' see you *once,*' says she, 'with a wee baby in your arms, as if 'twas your *own.* You'd look well. I'm thinkin'. Come, take un, Tim!'

"'Pass un over,' says he.

"She gave un the child. 'Well!' says she, throwin' up her little hands. 'You looks *perfectly* natural. Do he not, Mary? It might be his *own* for all one could tell. Why, Tim, you was *made* for the like o' that. Do it feel nice?'

"'Ay,' says poor Tim, from his heart. 'It do.'

"'Well, well!' says Polly. 'I 'low you're wishin', Tim, for one o' your own.'

"'I is.'

"Polly kissed the baby, then, an' rubbed it cheek t' cheek, so that her fluffy little head was close t' Tim. She looked up in his eyes. ''Tis a pity!' says she. An' she sighed.

"'Pity?' says he. 'Why, no!'

"'Poor lad!' says she. 'Poor lad!'

"'What's this!' says Tim. 'I've no cause for grief.'

"There was tears in little Polly's blue eyes as she took back the child. ''Tis a shame,' says she, 'that you've no child o' your own! An' you so wonderful fond o' children! I grieves for you, lad. It fair breaks my heart.'

"Some of the women laughed. An' this—somehow—moved Mary Mull t' vanish from that place.

"Well, now, Polly Twitter had worked her mischief. Mary Mull was never the same after that. She took t' the house. No church no more—no walkin' the roads. She was never seed abroad. An' she took t' tears an' broodin'. No ripple o' smiles no more—no song in the kitchen. She went downcast about the work o' the house, an' she sot overmuch alone in the twilight—an' she sighed too often—an' she looked too much at t' sea—an' she kep' silent too long—an' she cried too much in the night. She'd have nothin' t' do with children no more; nor would she let Tim Mull so much as lay a hand on the head of a youngster. Afore this, she'd never fretted for a child at all; she'd gone her way content in the world. But now—with Polly Twitter's vaunt forever in her ears—an' haunted by Tim Mull's wish for a child of his own—an' with the laughter o' the old women t' blister her pride—she was like t' lose her reason. An' the more it went on, the worse it got: for the folk o' the Tickle knowed very well that she'd give way t' envy an' anger, grievin' for what she couldn't have; an' she knowed that they knowed an' that they gossiped—an' this was like oil on a fire.

"'Tim,' says she, one night, that winter, 'will you listen t' me? Thinkin' things over, dear, I've chanced on a clever thing t' do. 'Tis queer, though.'

"'I'll not mind how queer, Mary.'

"She snuggled close to un, then, an' smiled. 'I wants t' go 'way from Tinkle Tickle,' says she.

"'Away from Tinkle Tickle?'

"'Don't say you'll not!'

"'Why, Mary, I was *born* here!'

"'I got t' go 'way.'

"'Wherefore?' says he. ''Tis good fishin' an' a friendly harbor.'

"'Oh, oh!' says she. 'I can't *stand* it no more.'

"'Mary, dear,' says he, 'there's no value in grievin' so sore over what can't be helped. Give it over, dear, an' be happy again, like you used t' be, won't you? Ah, now, Mary, won't you jus' try?'

"'I'm ashamed!'

"'Ashamed?' says he. 'You, Mary? Why, what's all this? There never was a woman so dear an' true as you.'

"'A childless woman! They mock me.'

"''Tis not true,' says he. 'They——'

"'Ay, 'tis true. They laugh. They whispers when I pass. I've heard un.'

"''Tis not true, at all,' says he. 'They loves you here at Tinkle Tickle.'

"'Oh, no, Tim! No, no! The women scoff. An' I'm ashamed. Oh, I'm ashamed t' be seen! I can't stand it no more. I got t' go 'way. Won't you take me, Tim?'

"Tim Mull looked, then, in her eyes. 'Ay,' says he, 'I'll take you, dear.'

" 'Not for long,' says she. 'Jus' for a year or two. T' some place where there's nobody about. I'll not want t' stay—so very long.'

" 'So long as you likes,' says he. 'I'm wantin' only t' see you well an' happy again. 'Tis a small thing t' leave Tinkle Tickle if we're t' bring about that. We'll move down the Labrador in the spring o' the year.' "

"In the spring o' the year I helped Tim Mull load his goods aboard a Labradorman an' close his cottage by Fo'c's'le Head.

" 'Spring weather, Tumm,' says he, 'is the time for adventure. I'm glad I'm goin'. Why,' says he, 'Mary is easin' off already.'

"Foreign for me, then. Spring weather; time for adventure. Genoa, this cruise, on a Twillingate schooner, with the first shore-fish. A Barbadoes cruise again. Then a v'y'ge out China way. Queer how the flea-bite o' travel will itch! An' so long as it itched I kep' on scratchin'. 'Twas over two years afore I got a good long breath o' the fogs o' these parts again. An' by this time a miracle had happened on the Labrador. The good Lord had surprised Mary Mull at Come-By-Guess Harbor. Ay, lads! At last Mary Mull had what she wanted. An' I had a godson. Tobias Tumm Mull had sot out on his cruise o' the seas o' this life. News o' all this cotched me when I landed at St. John's. 'Twas in a letter from Mary Mull herself.

"'Ecod!' thinks I, as I read; 'she'll never be content until she flaunts that child on the roads o' Tinkle Tickle.'

"An' 'twas true. 'Twas said so in the letter. They was movin' back t' Tinkle Tickle, says she, in the fall o' the year, t' live for good an' all. An' as for Tim, says she, a man jus' wouldn't believe how tickled he was.

"Me, too, ecod! I was tickled. Deep down in my heart I blessed the fortune that had come t' Mary Mull. An' I was fair achin' t' knock the breath out o' Tim with a clap on the back. 'Queer,' thinks I, 'how good luck may be delayed. An' the longer luck waits,' thinks I, 'the better it seems an' the more 'tis welcome.'

"'Twas an old letter, this, from Mary; 'twas near a year old. They was already back at Tinkle Tickle. An' so I laid in a silver spoon an' a silver mug, marked 'Toby' in fine fashion, against the time I might land at the Tickle. But I went clerk on the *Call Again* out o' Chain Harbor, that spring; an' 'twas not until midsummer that I got the chance t' drop in t' see how my godson was thrivin'. Lyin' here at Soap-an'-Water Harbor, one night, in stress o' weather, as now we lies here, I made up mind, come what might, that I'd run over t' Tinkle Tickle an' give the mug an' the spoon t' wee Toby when the gale should oblige us. 'July!' thinks I. 'Well, well! An' here it is the seventeenth o' the month. I'll drop in on the nineteenth an' help celebrate the first birthday o' that child. 'Twill be a joyous occasion by Fo'c's'le Head. An' I'll have the schooner decked out in her best, an' guns poppin'; an' I'll have Tim Mull aboard, when 'tis over, for a small nip o' rum.'

"But when Tim Mull come aboard at Tinkle Tickle t' greet me, I was fair aghast an' dismayed. Never afore had he looked so woebegone an' wan. Red eyes peerin' out from two black caves; face all screwed with anxious thought. He made me think of a fish-thief, somehow, with a constable comin' down with the wind; an' it seemed, too, that maybe 'twas my fish he'd stole. For he'd lost his ease; he was full o' sighs an' starts an' shifty glances. An' there was no health in his voice; 'twas but a disconsolate whisper—slinkin' out into the light o' day. 'Sin on his soul,' thinks I. 'He dwells in black weather.'

" 'We spied you from the head,' says he—an' sighed. 'It gives me a turn, lad, t' see you so sudden. But I'm wonderful glad you've come.'

" 'Glad?' says I. 'Then look glad, ye crab!' An' I fetched un a clap on the back.

" 'Ouch!' says he. 'Don't, Tumm!'

" 'I congratu*late* you,' says I.

"'Mm-m?' says he. 'Oh, ay! Sure, lad.' No smile, mark you. An' he looked off t' sea, as he spoke, an' then down at his boots, like a man in shame. 'Ay,' says he, brows down, voice gone low an' timid. 'Congratu*late* me, does you? Sure. That's proper—maybe.'

"'Nineteenth o' the month,' says I.

"'That's God's truth, Tumm.'

"'An' I'm come, ecod,' says I, 't' celebrate the first birthday o' Tobias Tumm Mull!'

"'First birthday,' says he. 'That's God's truth.'

"'Isn't there goin' t' *be* no celebration?'

"'Oh, sure!' says he. 'Oh, my, yes! Been gettin' ready for days. An' I've orders t' fetch you straightway t' the house. Supper's laid, Tumm. Four places at the board the night.'

"'I'll get my gifts,' says I; 'an' then——'

"He put a hand on my arm. 'What gifts?' says he.

"'Is you gone mad, Tim Mull?'

"'For—the child?' says he. 'Oh, sure! Mm-m!' He looked down at the deck. 'I hopes, Tumm,' says he, 'that they wasn't so very—expensive.'

"'I'll spend what I likes,' says I, 'on my own godson.'

"'Sure, you will!' says he. 'But I wish that——'

"Then no more. He stuttered—an' gulped—an' give a sigh—an' went for'ard. An' so I fetched the spoon an' the mug from below, in a sweat o' wonder an' fear, an' we went ashore in Tim's punt, with Tim as glum as a rainy day in the fall o' the year."

"An' now you may think that Mary Mull was woebegone, too. But she was not. Brown, plump, an' rosy! How she bloomed! She shone with health; she twinkled with good spirits. There was no sign o' shame upon her no more. Her big brown eyes was clean o' tears. Her voice was soft with content. A sweet woman, she was, ever, an' tender with happiness, now, when she met us at the threshold. I marveled that a gift like Toby Mull could work such a change in a woman. 'Tis queer how we thrives when we haves what we wants. She thanked me for the mug an' the spoon in a way that made me fair pity the joy that the little things give her.

"'For Toby!' says she. 'For wee Toby! Ah, Tumm, Tumm,—how wonderful thoughtful Toby's godfather is!"

"She wiped her eyes, then; an' I wondered that she should shed tears upon such an occasion—ay, wondered, an' could make nothin' of it at all.

"''Tis a great thing,' says she, 't' be the mother of a son. I lost my pride, Tumm, as you knows, afore we moved down the Labrador. But now, Tumm,—now, lad,—I'm jus' like other women. I'm jus' as much a woman, Tumm,' says she, 'as any woman o' Tinkle Tickle!'

"With that she patted my shoulder an' smiled an'

rippled with sweet laughter an' fled t' the kitchen t' spread Toby Mull's first birthday party.

" 'Tim,' says I, 'she've done well since Toby come.'

" 'Mm-m?' says he. 'Ay!'—an' smoked on.

" 'Ecod!' says I; 'she's blithe as a maid o' sixteen.'

" 'She's able t' hold her head up,' says he. 'Isn't afeared she'll be laughed at by the women no more. That's why. 'Tis simple.'

" 'You've lost heart yourself, Tim.'

" 'Me? Oh, no!' says he. 'I'm a bit off my feed. Nothin' more. An' I'm steadily improvin'. Steadily, Tumm,—improvin' steadily.'

" 'You've trouble, Tim?'

"He gripped his pipe with his teeth an' puffed hard. 'Ay,' says he, after a bit. 'I've trouble, Tumm. You got it right, lad.'

"Jus' then Mary Mull called t' supper. There was no time t' learn more o' this trouble. But I was bound an' determined, believe me, t' have Tim Mull aboard my craft, that night, an' fathom his woe. 'Twas a thousand pities that trouble should have un downcast when joy had come over the rim of his world like a new day."

"Places for four, ecod! Tim Mull was right. 'Twas a celebration. A place for Tim—an' a place for Mary—an' a place for me. An' there, too, was a place for Tobias Tumm Mull, a high chair, drawed close to his mother's side, with arms waitin' t' clutch an' hold the little nipper so soon as they fetched un in. I wished they'd not delay. 'Twas a strain on the patience. I'd long wanted—an' I'd come far—t' see my godson. But bein' a bachelor-man I held my tongue for a bit: for, thinks I, they're washin' an' curlin' the child, an' they'll fetch un in when they're ready t' do so, all spick-an'-span an' polished like a door-knob, an' crowin', too, the little rooster! 'Twas a fair sight to see Mary Mull smilin' beyond the tea-pot. 'Twas good t' see what she had provided. Cod's-tongues an' bacon—with new greens an' potatoes—an' capillaire-berry pie an' bake-apple jelly. 'Twas pretty, too, t' see the way she had arrayed the table. There was flowers from the hills flung about on the cloth. An' in the midst of all—fair in the middle o' the blossoms an' leaves an' toothsome plenty—was a white cake with one wee white taper burnin' as bright an' bold as ever a candle twice the size could manage.

"'Mary Mull,' says I, 'I've lost patience!'

"She laughed a little. 'Poor Tumm!' says she. 'I'm sorry your hunger had t' wait.'

"''Tis not my hunger.'

"She looked at me with her brow wrinkled. 'No?' says she.

"'I wants t' see what I've come t' see.'

"'That's queer!' says she. 'What you've come t' see?'

"'Woman,' cries I, "fetch in that baby!'

"Never a word. Never a sound. Mary Mull drawed back a step—an' stared at me with her eyes growin' wider an' wider. An' Tim Mull was lookin' out o' the window. An' I was much amazed by all this. An' then Mary Mull turned t' Tim. 'Tim,' says she, her voice slow an' low, 'did you not write Tumm a letter?'

"Tim faced about. 'No, Mary,' says he. 'I—I hadn't no time—t' waste with writin'.'

"'That's queer, Tim.'

"'I—I—I forgot.'

"'I'm sorry—Tim.'

"'Oh, Mary, I didn't *want* to!' says Tim. 'That's the truth of it, dear. I—I *hated*—t' do it.'

"'An' you said never a word comin' up the hill?'

"'God's sake!' cries Tim, like a man beggin' mercy, 'I *couldn't* say a word like that!'

"Mary turned then t' me. 'Tumm,' says she, 'little Toby—is dead.'

"'Dead, Mary!'

"'We didn't get much more than—jus' one good look at the little fellow—afore he left us.'

"When I took Tim Mull aboard the *Call Again* that night," the tale ran on, "'twas all clear above. What fog had been hangin' about had gone off with a little wind from the warm inland places. The lights o' Harbor—warm lights—gleamed all round about Black hills: still water in the lee o' the rocks. The tinkle of a bell fell down from the slope o' Lookout; an' a maid's laugh—sweet as the bell itself—come ripplin' from the shadows o' the road. Stars out; the little beggars kep' winkin' an' winkin' away at all the mystery here below jus' as if they knowed all about it an' was sure we'd be surprised when we come t' find out.

"'Tumm, ol' shipmate,' says Tim Mull, 'I got a lie on my soul.'

"''Tis a poor place for a burden like that.'

"'I'm fair wore out with the weight of it.'

"'Will you never be rid of it, man?'

"'Not an I keeps on bein' a man.'

"'So, Tim?'

"He put his hand on my shoulder. 'Is you a friend o' Mary's?' says he.

"''Tis a thing you must know without tellin'.'

"'She's a woman, Tumm.'

"'An' a wife.'

"'Woman an' wife,' says he, 'an' I loves her well, God knows!' The tinkle o' the bell on the black slope o' Lookout caught his ear. He listened —until the tender little sound ceased an' sleep fell again on the hill. 'Tumm,' says he, then, all at once, 'there never *was* no baby! She's deceivin' Tinkle Tickle t' save her pride!'"

Tumm closed the book he had read page by page.

VII

THE LITTLE NIPPER O' HIDE-AN'-SEEK HARBOR

VII

THE LITTLE NIPPER O' HIDE-AN'-SEEK HARBOR

WE nosed into Hide-an'-Seek Harbor jus' by chance. What come o' the venture has sauce enough t' tell about in any company that ever sot down in a forecastle of a windy night t' listen to a sentimental ol' codger like me spin his yarns. In the early dusk o' that night, a spurt o' foul weather begun t' swell out o' the nor'east—a fog as thick as soup an' a wind minded for too brisk a lark at sea. Hard Harry Hull 'lowed that we might jus' as well run into Hide-an'-Seek for a night's lodgin' in the lee o' the hills, an' pick up what fish we could trade the while, there bein' nothin' t' gain by hangin' off shore an' splittin' the big seas all night long in the rough. 'Twas a mean harbor, as it turned out—twelve score folk, ill-spoken of abroad, but with what justice none of us knowed; we had never dropped anchor there before. I was clerk o' the *Robin Red Breast* in them days—a fore-an'-aft schooner, tradin' trinkets an' grub for salt fish between Mother Burke o' Cape John an' the Newf'un'land ports o' the Straits o' Belle Isle; an' Hard Harry Hull, o' Yesterday Cove, was the skipper o' the craft. Ay, I means Hard Harry hisself—he that gained fame thereafter as a sealin' captain an' takes the *Queen o' the North* out o' St. John's t' the ice every spring o' the year t' this present.

Well, the folk come aboard in a twitter an' flutter o' curiosity, flockin' to a new trader, o' course, like young folk to a spectacle; an' they demanded my prices, an' eyed an' fingered my stock o' geegaws an' staples, an' they whispered an' stared an' tittered, an' they promised at last t' fetch off a quintal or two o' fish in the mornin', it might be, an the fog had blowed away by that time. 'Twas after dark afore they was all ashore again—all except a sorry ol' codger o' the name o' Anthony Lot, who had anchored hisself in the cabin with Skipper Harry an' me in expectation of a cup o' tea or the like o' that. By that time I had my shelves all put t' rights an' was stretched out on my counter, with my head on a roll o' factory-cotton, dawdlin' along with my friendly ol' flute. I tooted a ballad or two—Larboard Watch an' Dublin Bay; an' my fingers bein' limber an' able, then, I played the weird, sad songs o' little Toby Farr, o' Ha-ha Harbor, which is more t' my taste, mark you, than any o' the fashionable music that drifts our way from St. John's. Afore long I cotched ear of a foot-fall on deck—tip-toein' aft, soft as a cat; an' I knowed that my music had lured somebody close t' the cabin hatch t' listen, as often it did when I was meanderin' away t' ease my melancholy in the evenin'.

"On deck!" says Skipper Harry. "Hello, you!"

Nobody answered the skipper's hail. I 'lowed then that 'twas a bashful child I had lured with my sad melody.

"Come below," the skipper bawled, "whoever you is! I say—come below!"

"Isn't nobody there," says Anthony Lot.

"I heared a step," says I.

"Me, too," says Skipper Harry.

"Nothin' o' no consequence," says Anthony. "I wouldn't pay no attention t' that."

"Somebody up there in the rain," says the skipper.

"Oh, I knows who 'tis," says Anthony. " 'Tisn't nobody that amounts t' nothin' very much."

"Ah, well," says I, "we'll have un down here out o' the dark jus' the same."

"On deck there!" says the skipper again. "You is welcome below, sir!"

Down come a lad in response t' Hard Harry's hail—jus' a pallid, freckled little bay-noddie, with a tow head an' blue eyes, risin' ten years, or thereabouts, mostly skin, bones an' curiosity, such as you may find in shoals in every harbor o' the coast. He was blinded by the cabin lamp, an' brushed the light out of his eyes; an' he was abashed—less shy than cautious, however, mark you; an' I mind that he shuffled and grinned, none too sure of his welcome—halted, doubtful an' beseechin', like a dog on a clean kitchen floor. I marked in a sidelong glance, too, when I begun t' toot again, that his wee face was all in a pucker o' bewilderment, as he listened t' the sad strains o' Toby Farr's music, jus' as though he knowed he wasn't able t' rede the riddles of his life, jus' yet awhile, but would be able t' rede them, by an' by, when he growed up, an' expected t' find hisself in a pother o' trouble when he mastered the answers. I didn't know his name, then, t' be sure; had I knowed it, as know it I did, afore the night was over, I might have put down my flute, in amazement, an' stared an' said, "Well, well, well!" jus' as everybody did, no doubt, when they clapped eyes on that lad for the first time an' was told whose son he was.

"What's that wee thing you're blowin'?" says he.

"This here small contrivance, my son," says I, "is called a flute."

The lad scowled.

"Is she?" says he.

"Ay," says I, wonderin' wherein I had offended the wee feller; "that's the name she goes by in the parts she hails from."

"Hm-m," says he.

I seed that he wasn't thinkin' about the flute—that he was broodin'. All at once, then, I learned what 'twas about.

"I isn't your son," says he.

"That's true," says I. "What about it?"

"Well, you called me your son, didn't you?"

"Oh, well," says I, "I didn't mean——"

"What you do it for?"

'Twas a demand. The wee lad was stirred an' earnest. An' why? I was troubled. 'Twas a queer thing altogether. I seed that a man must walk warily in answer lest he bruise a wound. 'Twas plain that there was a deal o' delicate mystery beneath an' beyond.

"Answer me fair," says I, in banter; "wouldn't a man like me make a fair-t'-middlin' pa for a lad like you?"

That startled un.

"I'd wager no fish on it, sir," says he, "afore I learned more o' your quality."

"Well, then," says I, "you've but a dull outfit o' manners."

He flashed a saucy grin at me. 'Twas agreeable enough. I deserved it. An' 'twas made mild with a twinkle o' humor.

"I've pricked your pride, sir," says he. "I'm sorry."

"Answer me, then, in a mannerly way," says I, "Come now! Would I pass muster as a pa for a lad like you?"

He turned solemn an' earnest.

"You wish you was my pa?" says he.

"'Tis a sudden question," says I, "an' a poser."

"You doesn't, then?"

"I didn't say that," says I. "What you wishin' yourself?"

"I isn't wishin' nothin' at all about it," says he. "All I really wants to know is why you called me your son when I isn't no such thing."

"An' you wants an answer t' that?"

"I'd be grateful, sir."

Skipper Harry got the notion from all this talk, mixed with the eager, wistful look o' the lad, as he searched me with questions, t' ease the wonder that gripped an' hurt un, whatever it was—Skipper Harry got the notion that the lad had no father at all that he knowed of, an' that he sorrowed with shame on that account.

"I wish you was *my* son," says he, t' hearten un. "Danged if I don't!"

The lad flashed 'round on Skipper Harry an' stared at un with his eyes poppin'.

"What you say jus' then?" says he.

"You heared what I said."

"Say it again, sir, for my pleasure."

"I will," says the skipper, "an' glad to. I says I wish you belonged t' me."

"Is you sure about that?"

Skipper Harry couldn't very well turn back then. Nor was he the man t' withdraw. An' he didn't reef a rag o' the canvas he had spread in his kindly fervor.

"I is," says he. "Why?"

"It makes me wonder. What if you was my pa? Eh? What if you jus' happened t' be?"

"I'd be glad. That's what."

"That's queer!"

"Nothin' queer about it."

"Ah-ha!" says the lad; " 'tis wonderful queer!" He cocked his head an' peered at the skipper like an inquisitive bird. "Nobody never said nothin' like that t' me afore," says he. "What you wish I was your son for? Eh?"

"You is clever an' good enough, isn't you?"

"Maybe I is clever. Maybe I'm good, too. I'll not deny that I'm both. What I wants t' know, though, is what you wants me for?"

"I'd be proud o' you."

"What for?"

Skipper Harry lost patience.

"Don't pester me no more," says he. "I've no lad o' my own. That's reason enough."

The wee feller looked the skipper over from his shock o' red hair to his sea-boots, at leisure, an' turned doleful with pity.

"My duty, sir," says he. "I'm sore an' sorry for you."

"Don't you trouble about that."

"You sees, sir," says the lad, "I can't help you none. I got a pa o' my own."

"That's good," says the skipper. "I'm glad o' that."

"Moreover, sir," says the lad, "I'm content with

the pa I got. Yes, sir—I'm wonderful proud o' my pa, an' I 'low my pa's wonderful proud o' me, if the truth was knowed. I 'low not many lads on this coast is got such a wonderful pa as I got."

"No?" says I. "That's grand!"

"No, sir-ee! Is they, Anthony Lot?"

Anthony Lot begun t' titter an' chuckle. I fancied he cast a wink. 'Twas a broad joke he was playin' with, whatever an' all; an' I wished I knowed what amused the dolt.

"You got it right, Sammy," says he.

The lad slapped his knee. "Yes, sir-ee!" says he. "You jus' bet I got it right!"

"You got a wonderful ma, too?" says I.

"All I got is a wonderful pa," says he. "My ma died long, long ago. Didn't she, Anthony Lot? An' my pa's sailin' foreign parts jus' now. Isn't he, Anthony Lot? I might get a letter from un by the next mail-boat. No tellin' when a letter will come. Anytime at all—maybe next boat. An' my pa might turn up here hisself. Mightn't he, Anthony Lot? Might turn up right here in Hide-an'-Seek Harbor without givin' me the least word o' warnin'. Any day at all, too. Eh, Anthony Lot?"

"Skipper of a steam vessel in the South American trade," says Anthony.

"Any day at all?"

"Plyin' out o' Rio, I'm told."

"Eh, Anthony Lot? Any day at all?"

Anthony grinned at me in a way I'd no taste

for. "Any day at all," says he t' the lad. "You got it right, Sammy."

"Ol' Sandy Spot is fetchin' me up," says the lad, " 'til my pa comes home. It don't cost my pa a copper, neither. Ol' Sandy Spot is fetchin' me up jus' for my pa's sake. That's what comes o' havin' a pa like the pa I got. Don't it, Anthony Lot?"

"I 'low so, Sammy; jus' for your pa's sake—an' the Gov'ment stipend, too."

What slur was hid in that sly whisper about the Gov'ment stipend escaped the lad.

"Ah-ha!" he crowed.

I'm accustomed t' pry into the hearts o' folks. With no conscience at all I eavesdrops on feelin's. 'Tis a passion an' fixed practice. An' now my curiosity clamored for satisfaction. I was suspicious an' I was dumbfounded.

"You might put more heart in your crowin'," says I.

The lad turned on me with his breath caught an' his wee teeth as bare as a wolf's.

"What you say that for?" says he.

" 'Tis a pleasure," says I, "t' stir your wrath in your pa's behalf. 'Tis a pretty sight t' see. I enjoys it. In these modern times," says I, " 'tis not often I finds a lad as proud of his pa as you. My duty t' you, sir," says I. "I praise you."

The lad looked t' the skipper.

"My compliments," says Hard Harry, enjoyin' the play. "Me, too. I praise you highly."

"Whew!" says the lad. "Such manners abash me. There's no answer on the tip o' my tongue. I'm ashamed o' my wit."

Skipper Harry chuckled. An' I laughed. An' the wee lad laughed, too. An' dull Anthony Lot, in a fuddle o' stupidity an' wonder, stared from one t' the other, not knowin' whether t' grin or complain of our folly. There was foul weather without—wind in the riggin', blowin' in from the sea an' droppin' down over the hills, an' there was the patter o' black rain on the roof o' the cabin. 'Tis a matter for large surprise, it may be, that growed men, like Hard Harry an' me, should find interest an' laughter in a gossip like that. Yet 'tis dull times on a tradin' schooner, when trade's done for the day, an' the night's dismal an' sodden with rain; an' with a fire in the bogie-stove aboard, an' no lively maids t' draw un ashore to a dance or a scoff o' tea an' cakes in a strange harbor, a man seizes the distraction that seeks un out, and makes the best of it that he can. More than that, an' deep an' beyond it, 'twas entertainment, an' a good measure of it, that had come blinkin' down the deck. Afore we had time or cause for complaint o' the botheration o' childish company, we was involved in a brisk passage o' talk, which was no trouble at all, but sped on an' engaged us without pause. There was that about the wee lad o' Hide-an'-Seek Harbor, too, as a man sometimes encounters, t' command our interest an' t' compel our ears an' our tongues t' their labor.

With that, then, the lad's tongue broke loose an' ran riot in his father's praise. I never heared such wild boastin' in all my travels afore—eyes alight with pleasure, as I thought at the time, an' tow head waggin' with wonder an' pride, an' lips curlin' in contempt for the fathers of all the wide world in comparison; an' had not the lad been too tender in years for grave blame, too lonely an' forlorn for punishment, an' of a pretty loyalty to his father's fame and quality, pretty enough to excuse the preposterous tales that he told, I should have spanked un warmly, then an' there, an' bade un off ashore to cleanse his wee tongue o' the false inventions. There was no great deed that his father hadn't accomplished, no virtue he lacked, no piety he had not practiced; an' with every reckless, livin' boast o' the man's courage an' cleverness, his strength an' vast adventures, no matter how far-fetched, went a tale to enlighten an' prove it. The sea, the ice, the timber—'twas all the same; the father o' this lad was bolder an' wiser an' more gifted with graces than the fathers of all other lads—had endured more an' escaped more. So far past belief was the great tales the lad told that 'twas pitiable in the end; an' I wasn't quite sure—bein' a sentimental man—whether t' guffaw or t' blink with grief.

"You is spinnin' a wonderful lot o' big yarns

for a wee lad like you," says Skipper Harry. "Aw, now, an I was you," says he, in kindness, "I wouldn't carry on so careless."

"I knows other yarns."

"You s'prise me!"

"I could startle you more."

"Where'd you learn all them yarns?"

"I been told 'em."

"Your pa tell you?"

The lad laughed. "Dear man, no!" says he. "I never seed my pa in all my life."

"Never seed your pa in all your life! Well, now!"

"Why, no, sir! Didn't you know that?"

"You didn't tell me."

"I didn't think I *had* t' tell you. I thought ev'body in the world knowed that much about *me.*"

"Well, well!" says the skipper. "Never seed your pa in all your life! Who told you all them yarns then?"

"Ev'body."

"Oh! Ev'body, eh? I sees. Jus' so. You like t' hear yarns about your pa?"

"Well," says the lad, "I 'low I certainly do! Wouldn't you—if you had a pa like me?"

'Twas too swift a question.

"Me?" says Skipper Harry, nonplused.

"Ay—tell me!"

Skipper Harry was a kind man an' a foolish one.

"I bet ye I would!" says he, "I'd fair crave 'em. I'd pester the harbor with questions about my pa."

"That's jus' what I does do!" says the lad. "Doesn't I, Anthony Lot?"

"You got it right, Sammy," says Anthony. "You can't hear too much about your wonderful pa."

"You hears a lot, Sammy," says the skipper.

"Oh, ev'body knows my pa," says the lad, "an' ev'body spins me yarns about un."

"Jus' so," says the skipper, gone doleful. "I sees."

"Talkin' about my pa," says the lad, turnin' t' me, then, "I bet ye he could blow one o' them little black things better 'n you."

"He could play the flute, too!" says I.

"Well, I never been tol' so," says the lad; "but 'twould not s'prise me if he could. Could he, Anthony Lot?—could my pa play the flute?"

"He could."

"Better 'n this man?"

"Hoosh! Ay, that he could!"

"There!" says the lad. "I tol' you so!"

Anthony Lot turned his back on the lad an' cast a wink at me, an' grinned an' winked again, an' winked once more t' Skipper Harry; an' then he told us all as silly an' bitter cruel a whopper as ever I heared in all my travels. "Once upon a time, Sir Johnnie McLeod, him that was Gov'nor o' Newf'un'land in them days, sailed this coast in the Gov'ment yacht," says he; "an' when he come near by Hide-an'-Seek Harbor, he says: 'I've inspected this coast, an' I've seed the mines at Tilt Cove, an' the whale fishery at Sop's Arm, an' the mission at Battle Harbor, an' my report o' the wonders will mightily tickle His Gracious Majesty the King; but what I have most in mind, an' what lies nearest my heart, an' what I have looked forward to most of all, is t' sit down in my cabin, at ease, an' listen to a certain individual o' Hide-an'-Seek Harbor, which I heared about in England, play on the flute.' Well, the Gov'ment yacht dropped anchor in Hide-an'-Seek, Sammy, an' lied the night jus' where this here tradin' schooner lies now; an' when Sir Johnnie McLeod had heared your father play on the flute, he says: 'The man can play on the flute better 'n anybody in the whole world! I'm glad I've lived t' see this day. I'll see to it that he has a gold medal from His Gracious Majesty the King for this night's work.' "

"Did my pa get the gold medal from His Gracious Majesty?"

"He did, in due course."

"Ah-ha!" crowed the lad t' Skipper Harry. "I tol' you so!"

Skipper Harry's face had gone hard. He looked Anthony Lot in the eye until Anthony begun t' shift with uneasiness an' shame.

"Anthony," says he, "does that sort o' thing give you any real pleasure?"

"What sort o' thing?"

"Tellin' a yarn like that to a wee lad like he?"

" 'Twasn't nothin' wrong."

"Nothin' wrong!—t' bait un so?"

"Jus' a bit o' sport."

"Sorry sport!"

"Ah, well, he've growed used to it."

T' this the lad was listenin' like a caribou o' the barrens scentin' peril.

" 'Twas a naughty thing t' do, ye ol' crab!" says the skipper t' Anthony Lot.

The lad struck in.

"Isn't it true?" says he.

Skipper Harry cotched the quiver o' doubt an' fear in his voice an' was warned jus' in time. There was jus' one thing t' say.

"True?" says the skipper. "Sure, 'tis true! Who doubts it?"

"Not me," says Anthony.

"Ye hadn't better!" says the skipper.

"You bet ye 'tis true!" says I. "I've heared that selfsame tale many a time afore."

"Sammy, my son," says the skipper, "who is your father anyhow?"

The lad fair glowed with pride, as it seemed t' me then. Up went his head—out went his wee chest; an' his eyes went wide an' shinin', an' he smiled, an' the blood o' pride flushed his cheeks red.

"I'm John Scull's son!" says he.

Anthony Lot throwed back his head an' shot a laugh through his musty beard.

"Now," says he, "d'ye think it comical?"

Skipper Harry shook his head.

"God, no!" says he.

"What's the matter?" says the lad. His mouth was twitchin'. 'Twas awful t' behold. 'Tis worse when I think o' the whole truth of his state. "What's—what's the m-m-matter?" says he. "Wh-wh-what's the matter?"

Skipper Harry an' me jus' sot there starin' at un. John Scull's son! Everybody in Newf'un'land knowed all about John Scull o' Hide-an'-Seek Harbor.

'Twas plain—the whole tale o' the lad's little life. In all my travels afore I had never encountered a child in a state as woeful an' helpless as that. In the beginnin', no doubt, 'twas needful t' lie t' un—a baby, no more, bewildered by a mystery that he had now forgot all about, an' plyin' folk with questions in ease o' the desolation in which his father had plunged un. The folk o' Hide-an'-Seek Harbor had lied in kindness at first—'twas all plain; an' in the drift o' the years since then, little by little, more an' more, with less conscience all the while, they had lied for their own amusement. Look you, the lad had boasted, no doubt, an' was a comical sight when he did—chest out an' face scowlin' an' flushed, as we had seed it that night, an' his wee legs spread an' his way growed loud, whilst he declared the virtues of a father whose fortune was knowed to them all, young an' old alike, an' whose fate was a by-word. In the end, I'm thinkin', 'twas a cherished sport, followed by the folk o' the harbor an' all strangers, thus t' tell wild tales t' the lad, an' the wilder the more comical, of his father's great deeds; an' 'twas a better sport still, an' far more laughable, t' gather 'round un, at times, for their own amusement an' the entertainment o' travelers, an' hear un repeat, with his own small inventions t' season them, the whoppin' yarns they had teached un t' believe.

Skipper Harry was married to a maid o' Linger Tickle, an' was jus' a average, kindly sort o' man, with a heart soft enough, as the hearts o' most men is, t' be touched by the woes o' children, an' the will t' act rashly in relief o' them, come what might of it by an' by, if 'twas no hard riddle t' know what t' do at once. Sailin' our coast, I had heared un declare, poundin' it out on the forecastle table, that the man who debated a deed o' kindness with his own heart, or paused t' consider an' act o' punishment in company with his own reason, shamed his manhood thereby, an' fetched his soul into jeopardy. They called un Hard Harry, true enough; but 'twas not because his disposition was harsh—'twas because he was a hard driver at sea an' put the craft he was master of to as much labor as she could bear at all times. Knowin' the breed o' the man as well as I knowed it, I could tell that he was troubled, whether by wrath or grief, there was no knowin' which, an' would explode one way or t'other afore long. He must on deck for a fresh breath o' the wet night, says he, or smother; an' he would presently drop below again, says he, in command of his temper an' restlessness. I seed, too, that the lad wished t' follow—he watched the skipper up the ladder, like a doubtful dog, an' got up an' wagged hisself; but he thought better o' the intrusion an' set sail on another vast whopper in praise o' the father whose story we knowed.

When Skipper Harry come below again, he clapped a hand on Anthony Lot's shoulder in a way that jarred the man.

"Time you was stowed away in bed," says he.

Anthony took the hint. "I was jus' 'lowin' t' go ashore," says he. "You comin' along, Sammy?"

"I don't know," says Sammy. "I isn't quite tired of it here as yet."

"Well, now, I calls that complimentary!" says the skipper; "an' I'm inclined to indulge you. What say, Tumm? Mm-m? What say t' this here young gentleman?"

"I'm fond o' company," says I, "if 'tis genteel."

"Come, now, be candid!" says the skipper. "Is you suited with the company you is offered?"

" 'Tis genteel enough for me."

"Aw, you is jus' pokin' fun at me," says the lad. "I don't like it."

"I is not neither!" says I.

"I—I wish I could stay, sir," says Sammy t'

the skipper. "Jus', sir—jus' for a little small while. I—I——"

'Twas a plea. Skipper Harry cocked his ear in wonder. It seemed t' me that the lad had a purpose in mind.

"Well?" says the skipper.

The lad begun t' pant with a question, an' then, in a fright, t' lick his lips.

"Well, sir," says he, "I wants t' ask—I—I jus' got the notion t'——"

"Anthony," says the skipper, "your punt is frayin' the painter with eagerness t' be off t' bed."

With that Anthony went ashore.

"Now, son," says the skipper, "they're havin' a wonderful mug-up in the forecastle. You go for-'ard an' have a cup o' tea. 'Tis a cup o' tea that you wants, not the company o' me an' Mister Tumm, an' I knows it. You have a little scoff with the men, my son, an' then one o' the lads will put you ashore. You might come back for breakfast, too, an you is hungry again by that time."

"I'd as lief stay here," says Sammy.

"Oh, no," says the skipper; "you go for'ard an' have a nice cup o' tea with a whole lot o' white sugar in it."

"I'd like that."

"Sure, you would!"

"Is I t' have as much sugar as I wants?"

"You is, my son."

"May I tell the cook, sir, that 'tis by your leave an' orders?"

"Ay, my son."

The lad made t' go, with a duck of his head t' the skipper; but then he stopped an' faced about.

"Goin' t' turn in?" says he.

"No, son."

"By your leave, then," says the lad, "I'll be back t' bid you good night an' thank you afore I goes ashore."

"That's polite, my son. Pray do."

By this time the lad was skippin' up t' the deck an' Hard Harry was scowlin' with the trouble o' some anxious thought.

"Son!" says the skipper.

The lad turned.

"Sir?"

"An I was you," says Skipper Harry, "I wouldn't tell the lads up for'ard what my name was."

"You wouldn't?"

The skipper shook his head.

"Not me," says he.

"That's queer."

"Anyhow, I wouldn't."

"Why not, sir?"

"Oh, well, nothin' much," says the skipper. "You don't have to, do you? I 'low I jus' wouldn't do it. That's all."

The lad jumped into the cabin an' shook his wee fist in the skipper's face. "No, I don't have to," says he in a fury; "but I wants to, an' I will if I wants to! I'm not ashamed o' the name I wear!" An' he leaped up the ladder; an' when he had reached the deck, he turned an' thrust his head back, an' he called down t' the skipper, "Forgive my fault, sir!" An' then we heared his feet patter on the deck as he run for'ard.

Well, well, well, now, 'tis a sentimental tale, truly! I fears 'twill displease the majority—this long yarn o' the little mystery o' Hide-an-Seek Harbor. 'Tis a remarkable thing, I grant, t' thrust a wee lad like Sammy Scull so deep into the notice o' folk o' parts an' prominence; an' it may be, though I doubt it, that little codgers like he, snarled up in the coil o' their small lives, win no favor with the wealthy an' learned. I've told the tale more than once, never t' folk o' consequence, as now, occupied with affairs o' great gravity, with no time t' waste in the company o' far-away little shavers—I've never told the tale t' such folk at all, but only to the lowly of our coast, with the forecastle bogie warm of a windy night, an' the schooner hangin' on in the rain off the cliffs, or with us all settled afore a kitchen fire in a cottage ashore, of a winter's night, which is the most favorable hour, I've found out, for the tellin' o' tales like mine; an' the folk for whose pleasure I've spun this yarn have thought the fate o' wee Sammy worth their notice an' sighs, an' have thrilled me with wonder an' praise. I'm well warned that gentlefolk t' the s'uth'ard must have love in their tales an' be charmed with great deeds in its satisfaction; but I'm a skillful teller o' tales, as I've been told in high quarters, an' as I've good reason t' believe, indeed, with my own common sense and discretion t' clap me on the back, an' so I'll speed on with my sentimental tale to its endin', whether happy or not, an' jus' damn the scoffers in private.

"The little nipper," says the skipper. "His fist tapped the tip o' my nose!"

I laughed outright at that. 'Twas a good rebound from the start I had had.

"What stirred his wrath?"

"It might be one thing that I knows of," says I, "an' it might be another that I could guess."

"I'm puzzled, Tumm."

"As for me, I've the eyes of a hawk, sir," says I, "with which t' search a mystery like this."

"That you has!" says he.

I was fond o' Skipper Harry. He was a perceivin' man. An' I've no mind t' withhold the opinion I maintain t' that effect.

"You've fathomed the lad's rage?" says he.

"An I was still shrewder," says I, "I'd trust a surmise an' lay a wager that I was right."

"What do you think?"

"I've two opinions. They balance. I'll hold with neither 'til I'm sure o' the one."

"Not ashamed of his name!" says the skipper.

"Ha! 'Twas a queer boast t' make. He'll be ashamed of his name soon enough. 'Tis a wonder they've not told un the truth afore this. What you think, Tumm? How have they managed t' keep the truth from un until now?"

"They think un comical," says I; "they keeps un ignorant t' rouse their laughter with."

"Ay," says the skipper; "he've been fattened like a goose in a cage. They've made a sad fool of un these last few years. What boastin'! 'Tis stupid. He've growed old enough t' know better, Tumm. 'Tis jus' disgustin' t' hear a big boy like he mouth such a shoal o' foolish yarns. An' he've not the least notion that they're not as true as Gospel an' twice as entertainin'."

"So?" says I. "Where's my flute?"

"There'll come a time afore long when he'll find out all of a sudden about his pa. Whew!"

I found my flute an' stretched myself out on the counter t' draw comfort from tootin' it.

"Somebody'll blunder," says the skipper. "Some poor damn' fool."

"Is I ever played you Nellie was a Lady?"

" 'Tis awful!"

" 'Tis not," says I. " 'Tis a popular ballad an' has many good points."

"I don't mean the ballad, Tumm," says he. "Play it an you wants to. Don't sing it, though, I'm too bothered t' tolerate more confusion this night. The more I thinks o' the mess that that poor lad's in the worse I grieves. Man alive, 'tis a terrible business altogether! If they hadn't praised his father so high—if they hadn't teached the lad t' think that he'd write a letter or come home again—if the lad wasn't jus' the loyal little nipper that he is! I tell you, Tumm, that lad's sheer daft with admiration of his pa. He've lifted his pa above God Almighty. When he finds out the truth, he'll fall down and scream in agony, an' he'll die squirmin', too. I can fair hear un now—an' see un writhe in pain."

All this while I was whisperin' in my flute. 'Twas a comfort t' ease my mood in that way.

"I can't bear t' think of it, Tumm," says the skipper. " 'Tis the saddest thing ever I heared of. I wish we'd never dropped anchor in Hide-an'-Seek Harbor."

"I don't," says I.

"Then you've a heart harder than rock," says he.

"Come, now," says I; "have done with the matter. 'Tis no affair o' yours, is it?"

"The lad mustn't find out the truth."

"Can you stop the mouth o' the whole wide world?"

"You knows very well that I can't."

"I'm not so sure that 'twould be wise t' withhold the truth," says I. " 'Tis a mystery t' me—wisdom an' folly in a case like this. Anyhow," says I, givin' free course, in the melancholy that possessed me, to an impulse o' piety, "God Almighty knows how t' manage His world. An' as I looks at your face, an' as I listens t' your complaint," says I, "I'm willin' t' wager that He've got His plan worked near t' the point o' perfection at this very minute."

"Tell me how, Tumm."

"I'll leave you to brood on it," says I, "whilst I plays my flute."

Skipper Harry brooded whilst I tooted Toby Farr's woeful song called The Last Man o' the *Fore-an'-After:*

> When the schooner struck the rock,
> She was splintered by the shock;
>   An' the breakers didn't ask for leave or token.
> No! They hove un, man an' kid,
> Slap ag'in the cliff, they did,
>   An' kep' heavin' 'til the bones of all was broken!

"Skipper Harry," says I, then, puttin' aside my ol' flute, "doesn't you know what you can do t' help that lad out o' trouble for good an 'all?"

"I wish I did, Tumm."

"Is you as stupid as all that?"

"I isn't stupid as a usual thing," says he. "My wits is all scattered with rage an' sadness. That's the only trouble."

"Well," says I, "all you got t' do——"

Skipper Harry warned me.

"Hist!"

The lad was half way down the companion. I mind, as a man will recall, sometimes, harkin' back t' the crest an' close of a livin' tale like this poor yarn o' the little mystery o' Hide-an'-Seek Harbor, that there was wind in the riggin' an' black rain on the roof o 'the cabin. An' when I thinks of it all. as think of it I does, meanderin' along with my friendly ol' flute, of an evenin' in the fall o' the year, when trade's done an' the shelves is all put t' rights, I hears that undertone o' patter an' splash an' sigh. There was that in the lad's face t' stir an ache in the heart of a sentimental ol' codger like me; an' when I seed the grim lines an' gray color of it, an' when I caught the sorrow an' pride it uttered, as the lad halted, in doubt, peerin' at Skipper Harry in the hope of a welcome below, I knowed that my surmise was true. 'Twas a vision I had, I fancy—a flash o' revelation, such as may come, as some part o' the fortune they inherit, to habitual tellers o' tales o' the old an' young like me. A wee lad, true—Hide-an'-Seek born, an' fated the worst; yet I apprehended, all at once, the confusion he dwelt alone in, an' felt the weight o' the burden he carried alone; an' I must honor the courage an' good pride of his quality. Ay, I knows he was young! I knows that well enough! Nay, my sirs an' gentlefolk—I'm not makin' too much of it!

"Ah-ha!" says the skipper. "Here you is, eh? Come below, sir, an' feel welcome aboard."

Well, the lad come down with slow feet; an' then he stood before Skipper Harry like a culprit.

"Is you had your cup o' tea?" says the skipper.

"Yes, sir. I thanks you, sir, for my cup o' tea."

"Sugar in it?"

"Yes, sir."

"All you wanted?"

"As much as my need, sir, an' more than my deserts."

Skipper Harry clapped un on the back.

"All nonsense!" says he. "You're no judge o' your deserts. They're a good round measure, I'll be bound!"

"They isn't, sir."

"No more o' that! You is jus' as worthy——"

"No, I isn't!"

"Well, then, have it your own way," says the skipper. "Is you comin' back for breakfast in the mornin'? That's what I wants t' know."

"No, sir."

Skipper Harry jumped.

"What's that?" says he. "Why not?"

"I've shamed your goodness, sir."

"Bosh!" says the skipper.

The lad's lips was dry. He licked 'em. An' his throat was dry. He gulped. An' his voice was hoarse.

"I been lyin' t' you," says he.

"You been——"

All at once the lad's voice went shrill as a maid's. 'Twas distressful t' hear.

"Lyin' t' you, sir!" says he. "I been lyin' t' you jus' like mad! An' now you'll not forgive me!"

"Tumm," says the skipper, "this is a very queer thing. I can't make it out."

I could.

"No harm in easin' the conscience freely," says I t' the lad. "What you been lyin' about?"

"Heed me well, sir!" This t' the skipper.

"Ay, my son?"

"I isn't got no pa! My pa's dead! My pa was hanged by the neck until he was dead for the murder o' Mean Michael Mitchell o' Topsail Run!"

Well, that was true. Skipper Harry an' me knowed that. Everybody in Newf'un'land knowed it. Seven years afore—the hangin' was done. Sammy Scull was a baby o' three at the time. 'Twas a man's crime, whatever, if a man an' a crime can be linked with satisfaction. Still an' all, 'twas a murder, an' a foul, foul deed for that reason. We've few murders in Newf'un'land. They shock us. They're never forgotten. An' there was a deal made o' that one, an' 'twas still the latest murder—news o' the trial at St. John's spread broadcast over the three coasts; an' talk o' the black cap an' the black flag, an' gruesome tales o' the gallows an' the last prayer, an' whispers o' the quicklime that ended it all. Sammy Scull could go nowhere in Newf'un'land an' escape the shadow an' shame o' that rope. Let the lad grow t' manhood? No matter. Let un live it down? He could not. The tongues o' the gossips would wag in his wake wheresoever he went. Son of John Scull o' Hide-an'-Seek Harbor! Why, sir, the man's father was hanged by the neck at St. John's for the murder o' Mean Michael Mitchell o' Topsail Run!

Skipper Harry put a hand on Sammy Scull's head.

"My son," says he, "is you quite sure about what you've jus' told us?"

"Yes, sir."

"How long is you knowed it?"

"Oh, a long, long time, sir! I learned it of a dirty day in the fall o' last year. Isn't it—isn't it true, sir?"

Skipper Harry nodded.

"Ay, my son," says he; " 'tis quite true."

"Oh, my poor pa!"

Skipper Harry put a finger under the lad's chin an' tipped up his face.

"Who tol' you?" says he.

"I found a ol' newspaper, sir, in Sandy Spot's bureau, sir, where I was forbid t' pry, sir, an' I read all about it. My pa left one child named Samuel when he was hanged by the neck—an' that's me."

"You've told nobody what you learned?"

"No, sir."

"Why not?"

"I'd liefer pretend not t' know, sir, when they baited me, an' so save myself shame."

"Jus' so, my son."

"An' I jus' lied an' lied an' lied!"

"Mm-m."

Skipper Harry lifted the lad t' the counter, then, an' bent to a level with his eyes.

"Look me in the eye, son," says he. "I've a grave word t' say t' you. Will you listen well an' ponder?"

"I'll ponder, sir, an you'll jus' forgive my fault."

"Sammy, my son," says the skipper, "I forgives it freely. Now, listen t' me. Is you listenin'? Well, now, I knows a snug harbor t' the south o' this. 'Tis called Yesterday Cove. An' in the harbor is a cottage, an' in the cottage is a woman; an' the woman is ample an' kind. She've no lad of her own—that kind, ample woman. She've only a husband. That's me. An' I been thinkin'——"

I stirred myself.

"I 'low I'll meander for'ard," says I, "an' have a cup o' tea with the hands."

"Do, Tumm," says the skipper.

Well, now, I went for'ard t' have my cup o' tea an' brood on this sorry matter. 'Twas plain, however, what was in the wind; an' when I went aft again, an' begun t' meander along, breathin' the sad strains o' Toby Farr's songs on my flute, the thing had come t' pass, though no word was said about it. There was the skipper an' wee Sammy Scull, yarnin' t'gether like ol' cronies—the lad with his ears an' eyes wide t' the tale that Hard Harry was tellin'. I jus' wet my whistle with a drop o' water, t' limber my lips for the music, an' whispered away on my flute; but as I played I must listen, an' as I listened I was astonished, an' presently I give over my tootin' altogether, the better t' hearken t' the wild yarn that Hard Harry was spinnin'. 'Twas a yarn that was well knowed t' me. Man alive! Whew! 'Twas a tax on the belief—that yarn! Ay, I had heared it afore—the yarn o' how Hard Harry had chopped a way t' the crest of an iceberg in foul weather t' spy out a course above the fog, an' o' how he had split the berg in two with the last blow of his ax, an' falled safe between the halves, an' swimmed aboard his schooner in a gale o' wind; an' though I had heared the tale verified by others, I never could swallow it whole at all, but deemed it the cleverest whopper that ever a man had invented in play.

When Skipper Harry had done, the lad turned t' me, his face in a flush o' pride.

"Mister Tumm!" says he.

"Sir t' you?" says I.

"Is you listenin' t' me?"

"I is."

"Well, then, you listen an' learn. That's what I wants *you* t' do."

"I'll learn all I can," says I. "What is it?"

Sammy Scull slapped his knee. An' he laughed

a free ripple o' glee an' looked Skipper Harry over whilst he vowed the truth of his words. "I'll lay my liver an' lights on it," says he, "that I got the boldest pa . . ."

That's all.

VIII

SMALL SAM SMALL

VIII

SMALL SAM SMALL

WE were lying snug from the wind and sea in Right-an'-Tight Cove—the Straits shore of the Labrador—when Tumm, the clerk of the *Quick as Wink,* trading the northern outports for salt cod in fall weather, told the engaging tale of Small Sam Small, of Whooping Harbor. It was raining. This was a sweeping downpour, sleety and thick, driving, as they say in those parts, from a sky as black as a wolf's throat. There was no star showing; there were cottage lights on the hills ashore—warm and human little glimmers in the dark—but otherwise a black confusion all round about. The wind, running down from the north-west, tumbled over the cliff, and swirled, bewildered and angry, in the lee of it. Riding under Lost Craft Head, in this black turmoil, the schooner shivered a bit; and she droned aloft, and she whined below, and she restlessly rose and fell in the soft swell that came spent and frothy from the wide open through Run Away Tickle. But for all we in the forecastle knew of the bitter night—of the roaring white seas and a wind thick and stinging with spume snatched from the long crests—it was blowing a moonlit breeze aboard. The forecastle lamp burned placidly; and the little stove was busy with its accustomed employment—laboring with much noisy fuss in the display of its genial accomplishments. Skipper and crew—and Tumm, the clerk, and I—lounged at ease in the glow and warmth. No gale from the nor'west, blow as it would in fall weather, could trouble the *Quick as Wink,* lying at anchor under Lost Craft Head in Right-an'-Tight Cove of the Labrador.

"When a man lays hold on a little strand o' human wisdom," said Tumm, breaking a heavy muse, "an' hangs his whole weight to it," he added, with care, "he've no cause t' agitate hisself with surprise if the rope snaps."

"What's *this* preachin'?" the skipper demanded.

"That ain't no preachin'," said Tumm, resentfully; " 'tis a *fact.*"

"Well," the skipper complained, "what you want t' go an' ask a hard question like that for?"

"Sittin' here in the forecastle o' the ol' *Quick as Wink,* in this here black gale from the nor'west," said Tumm, "along o' four disgruntled dummies an' a capital P passenger in the doldrums, I been thinkin' o' Small Sam Small o' Whoopin' Harbor. 'This here world, accordin' as she's run,' says Small Sam Small, 'is no fit place for a decent man t' dwell. The law o' life, as I was teached it,' says he, 'is *Have;* but as I sees the needs o' men, Tumm, it ought t' be *Give.* T' *have*—t' *take* an' t' *keep*—breaks a good man's heart in the end. He lies awake in the night, Tumm—in the company of his own heart—an' he isn't able t' forget jus' how he *got.* I'm no great admirer o' the world, an' I isn't very fond o' life,' says he; 'but I knows the law o' life, an' lives the best I can accordin' t' the rules I've learned. I was cast out t' make my way as a wee small lad; an' I was teached the law o' life by harsh masters—by nights' labor, an' kicks, an' robbery, Tumm, by wind, an' cold, an' great big seas, by a empty belly, an' the fear o' death in my small heart. So I'm a mean man. I'm the meanest man in Newf'un'land. They says my twin sister died o' starvation at the age o' two months along o' my greed. May be: I don't know—but I hopes I never was born the mean man I is. Anyhow,' says he, 'Small Sam Small—that's me—an' I stands by! I'm a damned mean man, an' I isn't unaware; but they isn't a man on the St. John's waterside—an' they isn't a big-bug o' Water Street—can say t' *me,* "Do this, ye bay-noddie!" or, "Do that, ye bankrupt out-porter!" or, "Sign this, ye coast's whelp!" Still an' all, Tumm,' says he, 'I don't like myself very much, an' I isn't very fond o' the company o' the soul my soul's become.'

"'Never you mind, Sam Small,' says I; 'we've all done dirty tricks in our time.'

"'All?'

"'Never a mother's son in all the world past

fourteen years,' says I, 'hasn't a ghost o' wicked conduct t' haunt his hours alone.'

"'You, too, Tumm?'

"'*Me?*' says I. 'Good Heavens!'

"'Uh-huh,' says he. 'I 'low; but that don't comfort *me* so very much. You see, Tumm, I got t' live with myself, an' bein' quite well acquainted with myself, I don't *like* to. They isn't much domestic peace in my ol' heart; an' they isn't no divorce court I ever heared tell of, neither here nor hereafter, in which a man can free hisself from his own damned soul.'

"'Never you mind,' says I.

"'Uh-huh,' says he. 'You see, I *don't* mind. I—I—I jus' don't *dast!* But if I could break the law, as I've been teached it,' says he, 'they isn't nothin' in the world I'd rather do, Tumm, than found a norphan asylum.'

"'Maybe you will,' says I.

"'Too late,' says he; 'you see, I'm fashioned.'

"He was."

Tumm laughed a little.

Tumm warned us: "You'll withhold your pity for a bit, I 'low. 'Tis not yet due ol' Small Sam Small." He went on: "Small? An'—an' ecod! Small Sam Small! He gained the name past middle age, they says, long afore I knowed un; an' 'tis a pretty tale, as they tells it. He skippered the *Last Chance*—a Twillingate fore-an'-after, fishin' the

Labrador, hand an' trap, between the Devil's Battery an' the Barnyards—the Year o' the Third Big Haul. An' it seems he fell in love with the cook. God save us! Sam Small in love with the cook! She was the on'y woman aboard, as it used t' be afore the law was made for women; an' a sweet an' likely maid, they says—a rosy, dimpled, good-natured lass, hailin' from down Chain Tickle way, but over-young an' trustful, as it turned out, t' be voyagin' north t' the fishin' with the likes o' Small Sam Small. A hearty maid, they says—blue-eyed an' flaxen—good for labor an' quick t' love. An' havin' fell in love with her, whatever, Small Sam Small opened his heart for a minute, an' give her his silver watch t' gain her admiration. 'You'll never tell the crew, my dear,' says he, 'that I done such a foolish thing!' So the maid stowed the gift in her box—much pleased, the while, they says, with Small Sam Small—an' said never a word about it. She'd a brother t' home, they says—a wee bit of a chappie with a lame leg—an' thinks she, 'I'll give Billy my silver watch.'

"But Sam Small, bein' small, repented the gift; an' when the *Last Chance* dropped anchor in Twillingate harbor, loaded t' the gunwales with green fish, he come scowlin' on deck.

" 'They isn't none o' you goin' ashore yet,' says he.

" 'Why not?' says they.

" 'They isn't none o' you goin' ashore,' says he, 'afore a constable comes aboard.'

" 'What you wantin' a constable for?' says they.

" 'They isn't none o' you goin' ashore afore this schooner's searched,' says he. 'My silver watch is stole.'

" 'Stole!' says they.

" 'Ay,' says he; 'somebody's took my silver watch.' "

Tumm paused.

"Tumm," the skipper of the *Quick as Wink* demanded, "what become o' that there little maid from Chain Tickle?"

"Well," Tumm drawled, "the maid from Chain Tickle had her baby in jail. . . .

"You see," Tumm ran along, in haste to be gone from this tragedy, "Sam Small *was* small—almighty small an' mean. A gray-faced ol' skinflint—an' knowed for such: knowed from Chidley t' Cape Race an' the Newf'un'land Grand Banks as the meanest wolf the Almighty ever made the mistake o' lettin' loose in a kindly world—knowed for the same in every tap-room o' the St. John's water-side, from the Royal George t' the Anchor an' Chain—a lean, lanky, hunch-shouldered, ghastly ol' codger in Jews' slops an' misfits, with a long white beard, a scrawny neck, lean chops, an' squintin' little eyes, as green an' cold as an iceberg in gray weather. Honest or dishonest?—ecod! what matter? They's nothin' so wicked as meanness. But the law hadn't cotched un: for the law winks with both eyes. 'I'm too old for crime now, an' too rich,' says he; 'but I've worked hard, accordin' t' the law o' life, as she was teached me, an' I've took chances in my time. When I traveled the outports in my youth,' says he, 'I sold liquor for green paint an' slep' with the constable; an' the socks o' the outport fishermen, Tumm,' says he, 'holds many a half-dollar I coined in my Whoopin' Harbor days.' He'd no piety t' save his soul. 'No church for me,' says he; 'you see, I'm no admirer o' the handiwork o' God. Git, keep, an' have,' says he; 'that's the religion o' my youth, an' I'll never despite the teachin' o' them years.' Havin' no bowels o' compassion, he'd waxed rich in his old age. 'Oh,' says he, 'I'm savin' along, Tumm—I'm jus' savin' along so-so for a little job I got t' do.' Savin' along? He'd two schooners fishin' the Labrador in the season, a share in a hundred-ton banker, stock in a south coast whale-factory, God knows how much yellow gold in the bank, an' a round interest in the swiler *Royal Bloodhound,* which he skippered t' the ice every spring o' the year.

"'So-so,' says he; 'jus' savin' along so-so.'

"'So-so!' says I; 'you're *rich,* Skipper Sammy.'

"'I'm not jus' in agreement with the plan o' the world as she's run,' says he; 'but if I've a fortune t' ease my humor, I 'low the Lord gets even, after all.'

" 'How so?' says I.

" 'If I'm blessed with a taste for savin', Tumm,' says he, 'I'm cursed with a thirst for liquor.'

" 'Twas true enough, I 'low. The handiwork o' God, in the matter o' men's hearts, is by times beyond me t' fathom. For look you! a poor devil will want This an' crave That when This an' That are spittin' cat an' growlin' dog. They's small hope for a man's peace in a mess like that. A lee shore, ecod!—breakers t' le'ward an' a brutal big wind jumpin' down from the open sea. Thirst an' meanness never yet kep' agreeable company. 'Tis a wonderful mess, ecod! when the Almighty puts the love of a penny in a mean man's heart an' tunes his gullet t' the appreciation o' good Jamaica rum. An' I never knowed a man t' carry a more irksome burden of appetite than Small Sam Small o' Whoopin' Harbor. 'Twas fair horrible t' see. Cursed with a taste for savin', ay, an' cursed, too, with a thirst for good Jamaica rum! I've seen his eyes glitter an' his tongue lick his lips at the sight of a bottle; an' I've heared un groan, an' seed his face screw up, when he pinched the pennies in his pocket an' turned away from the temptation t' spend. It hurt un t' the backbone t' pull a cork; he squirmed when his dram got past his Adam's apple. An', Lord! how the outport crews would grin t' see un trickle little drops o' liquor into his belly—t' watch un shift in his chair at the Anchor an' Chain, an' t' hear un grunt an' sigh when the dram was down.

But Small Sam Small was no toper. Half-seas-over jus' on'y once. It cost un dear.

"I sailed along o' Cap'n Sammy," Tumm resumed, "on the swilin' v'yage in the spring o' the Year o' the Westerly Gales. I mind it well: I've cause. The *Royal Bloodhound:* a stout an' well-found craft. An' a spry an' likely crew: Sam Small never lacked the pick o' the swilin'-boys when it come t' fittin' out for the ice in the spring o' the year. He'd get his load o' fat with the cleverest skippers of un all; an' the wily skippers o' the fleet would tag the ol' rat through the ice from Battle Harbor t' the Grand Banks. 'Small Sam Small,' says they, 'will nose out them swiles.' An' Small Sam Small done it every spring o' the year. No clothes off for Small Sam Small! 'Twas tramp the deck, night an' day. 'Twas 'How's the weather?' at midnight an' noon. 'Twas the crow's-nest at dawn. 'Twas squintin' little green eyes glued t' the glass the day long. An' 'twas 'Does you see un, lads?' forever an' all; an' 'twas *'Damme, where's that fat?'* But 'twas now Sam Small's last v'yage, says he; he'd settle down when he made port again, an' live free an' easy in his old age, with a good fire t' warm his bones, an' a bottle at his elbow for reasonable sippin' of a cold night. A man should loosen up in his old age, says he; an' God grantin' him bloody decks an' a profitable slaughter, that v'yage, he'd settle down for good an' never leave port again. He was tired, says he; he was old—an' he was all tired out—and he'd use the comfort he'd earned in all them years o' labor an' savin'. Wasn't so much in life, after all, for a old man like him, says he, except a fireside chair, or a seat in the sunlight, with a nip o' the best Jamaica, watered t' the taste.

" 'You come along o' me as mate, Tumm,' says he, 'an' I'll fill your pocket.'

" 'I'm not averse t' cash,' says I.

" 'These here ol' bones creaks out t' the ice for *swiles,*' says he, 'an' not for the pleasures o' cruisin'.'

" 'I'll ship, Skipper Sammy,' says I. 'I'll ship with the skipper that gets the fat.'

" 'You hails from Chain Tickle?' says he.

" 'I does.'

" 'Tumm,' says he, 'I'm a old man, an' I'm downcast in these last days; an' I been 'lowin', somehow, o' late, that a dash o' young blood in my whereabouts might cheer me up. I 'low, Tumm,' says he, 'you don't know a likely lad t' take along t' the ice an' break in for his own good? Fifteen years or so? I'd berth un well aboard the *Bloodhound.*'

" 'I does,' says I.

" 'You might fetch un,' says he; 'nothin' like young blood t' cheer the aged.'

" 'I'll fetch un quick enough, Skipper Sammy,' says I, 'if you'll stand by my choice.'

" 'As I knowed you would, Tumm,' says he, 'you takes me cleverly.'

"It wasn't long after that afore a young lad I knowed in Chain Tickle come shoutin' down t' St. John's. A likely lad, too: blue-eyed, tow-headed, an' merry—the likes of his mother, a widow. No liar, no coward, no pinch-a-penny: a fair, frank-eyed, lovable little rascal—a forgiven young scape-grace—with no mind beyond the love an' livin' jollity o' the day. Hang the morrow! says he; the morrow might do very well, he'd be bound, when it come. Show *him* the fun o' the minute. An' he had a laugh t' shame the dumps—a laugh as catchin' as smallpox. 'Ecod!' thinks I; 'it may very well be that Sam Small will smile.' A brave an' likely lad: with no fear o' the devil hisself—nor overmuch regard, I'm thinkin', for the chastisements o' God Almighty—but on'y respect for the wish of his own little mother, who was God enough for he. 'What!' says he; 'we're never goin' t' sea with Sam Small. Small Sam Small? Sam Small, the skinflint?' But he took a wonderful fancy t' Small Sam Small; an' as for Skipper Sammy—why—Skipper Sammy loved the graceless rogue on sight. 'Why, Tumm,' says he, 'he's jus' like a gentleman's son. Why 'tis—'tis like a nip o' rum—'tis as good as a nip o' the best Jamaica—t' clap eyes on a fair, fine lad like that. Is you marked his eyes, Tumm?—saucy as blood an' riches. They fair bored me t' the soul like Sir Harry McCracken's. They's blood behind them eyes—blood an' a sense o' wealth. An' his strut! Is you marked the strut,

Tumm?—the very air of a game-cock in a barnyard. It takes a gentleman born t' walk like that. I tells you, Tumm, with wealth t' back un—with wealth t' back body an' brain an' blue blood like that—the lad would be a lawyer at twenty-three an' Chief Justice o' Newf'un'land at thirty-seven. You mark *me!*'

"I'm thinkin', whatever, that Small Sam Small had the natural prejudice o' fatherhood.

" 'Tumm,' says he, 'he's cheered me up. Is he savin'?'

" 'Try for yourself,' says I.

"Skipper Sammy put the boy t' the test, next night, at the Anchor an' Chain. 'Lad,' says he, 'here's the gift o' half a dollar.'

" 'For *me,* Skipper Sammy?' says the lad. ' 'Tis as much as ever I had in my life. Have a drink.'

" 'Have a *what?*'

" 'You been wonderful good t' me, Skipper Sammy,' says the lad, 'an' I wants t' buy you a glass o' good rum.'

" 'Huh!' says Small Sam Small; ' 'tis expensive.'

" 'Ay,' says the lad; 'but what's a half-dollar *for?*'

" 'Well,' says Skipper Sammy, 'a careful lad like you *might* save it.'

"The poor lad passed the half-dollar back over the table t' Small Sam Small. 'Skipper Sammy,' says he, '*you* save it. It fair burns my fingers.'

" 'Mary, my dear,' says Sam Small t' the barmaid, 'a couple o' nips o' the best Jamaica you got in the house for me an' Mr. Tumm. Fetch the lad a bottle o' ginger-ale—*im*-ported. Damn the expense, anyhow! Let the lad spend his money as he has the notion.'

"An' Sam Small smiled.

"'Tumm,' says Small Sam Small, that night, when the boy was gone t' bed, 'ecod! but the child spends like a gentleman.'

"'How's that, Skipper Sammy?'

"'Free,' says he, 'an' genial.'

"'He'll overdo it,' says I.

"'No,' says he; ''tisn't in the blood. He'll spend what he haves—no more. An' like a gentleman, too —free an' genial as the big-bugs. A marvelous lad, Tumm,' says he; 'he've ab-se-*lute*-ly no regard for money.'

"'Not he.'

"'Ecod!'

"'He'll be a comfort, Skipper Sammy,' says I, 'on the swilin' v'yage.'

"'I 'low, Tumm,' says he, 'that I've missed a lot, in my life, these last fifteen year, through foolishness. You send the lad home,' says he; 'he's a gentleman, an' haves no place on a swilin'-ship. An' they isn't no sense, Tumm,' says he, 'in chancin' the life of a fair lad like that at sea. Let un go home to his mother; *she'll* be glad t' see un again. A man ought t' loosen up in his old age: I'll pay. An', Tumm—here's a two-dollar note. You tell the lad t' waste it *all* on bananas. This here bein' generous,' says he, 'is an expensive diversion. I got t' save my pennies—*now!*'

"Well, well!" Tumm went on; "trust Small Sam Small t' be off for the ice on the stroke o' the hour for swilers' sailin'—an' a few minutes t' win'ward o' the law. An' the *Royal Bloodhound* had heels, too—an' a heart for labor. With a fair start from Seldom-Come-By, Skipper Sammy beat the fleet t' the Funks an' t' the first drift-ice beyond. March days: nor'westerly gales, white water an' snowy weather—an' no let-up on the engines. Ice? Ay; big floes o' northerly ice, come down from the Circle with current an' wind—breedin'-grounds for swile. But there wasn't no swiles. Never the bark of a dog-hood nor the whine of a new-born white-coat. Cap'n Sammy nosed the ice into White Bay; he worked out above the Horse Islands; he took a peep at the Cape Norman light an' swatched the Labrador seas. But never a swile got we. 'The swiles,' says he, 'is t' the east an' s'uth'ard. With these here westerly gales blowin' wild an' cold as perdition they've gone down the Grand Banks way. The fleet will smell around here till they wears their noses out,' says he; 'but Cap'n Sam Small is off t' the s'uth'ard t' get his load o' fat.' An' he switched the *Royal Bloodhound* about, an' steamed off, with all sail spread, bound down t' the Grand Banks in a nor'west gale, with a burst o' snow t' season it.

"We made the northerly limits o' the Grand Banks in fog an' ca'm weather. Black fog: thick 's mud. We lay to—butted a league into the pack-ice. Greasy weather: a close world an' a moody glass.

" 'Cap'n Sammy,' says I, on the bridge, 'there's no tellin' where a man will strike the fat.'

" 'Small chance for fat, damme!' says he, 'in fog an' broodin' weather.'

" 'Give her a show,' says I, 'an' she'll lighten.'

" 'Lighten?' says he. 'Afore night, Tumm, she'll blow this fog t' the Saragossa Sea.'

"The glass was in a mean, poor temper, an' the air was still, an' thick, an' sweaty.

" 'Blow?' says he. 'Ay; she's breedin' a naughty nor'west gale o' wind down there.'

"It seemed t' me then I seed a shadow in the fog; an', 'Cap'n Sammy,' says I, 'what's that off the port bow?'

" 'What's what?' says he.

" 'That patch o' black in the mist.'

" 'Tumm,' says he, 'you might tweak the toot-rope.'

"The *Royal Bloodhound* hadn't opened her mouth afore there came a howl from the mist.

"Cap'n Sammy jumped. 'What d'ye make o' that?' says he.

" 'I make a ship,' says I.

"He lifted his hand. 'Hark!' says he.

"Whatever she was, she was yellin' for help like a bull in a bog.

"'Whoo-o-o-oo! Whoo, whoo! Whoo-o-oo-*ugh!*'

"Cap'n Sammy grinned. 'I make a tramp cotched fast in the ice,' says he.

"'Whoo-o-oo-*ugh!* Whoo, whoo, whoo, whoo-o-*oop!*'

"'I make a tramp,' says he, rubbin' his hands, 'with her propeller ripped off.'

"I reached a hand for the rope.

"'Hol' on!' says he; 'you keep your hook off that there whistle.'

"'I was thinkin',' says I, 't' speed a message o' comfort.'

"'Let her beller a bit, ye dunderhead!' says he.

"'What for?' says I.

"'T' make sure in her own mind,' says he, 'that she needs a kindly hand t' help her.'

"'Twould be easy enough for the steam-swiler *Royal Bloodhound* t' jerk that yelpin' tramp, had she lost her propeller—as well she might, poor helpless lady o' fashion! in that slob-ice—'twould be easy enough t' rip her through a league o' the floe t' open water, with a charge or two o' good black powder t' help.

"'Tumm,' says Cap'n Sammy, by an' by, 'how's the glass?'

"'She've the look an' conduct o' the devil, sir.'

"'Good!' says he. 'I hopes she kicks the bottom

out. You might go so far as t' give that bellerin' ironclad a toot.'

"I tooted.

"'You come along o' me, Tumm,' says he, 'an' learn how t' squeeze a lemon.'

"Cap'n Sammy kep' explodin' in little chuckles, like a bunch o' Queen's-birthday firecrackers, as we trudged the ice toward the howlin' ship in the mist. 'Twas a hundred fathoms o' rough goin', I promise you, that northern slob, in which the tramp an' the *Royal Bloodhound* lay neighbors; an' 'twas mixed with hummocks an' bergs, an' 'twas all raftered an' jammed by the westerly gales o' that season. After dawn then; an' 'twas a slow, greasy dawn, I mind. But the yellow light growed fast in the fog; an' the mist thinned in a whiff o' wind from the nor'west. 'Twould lift, by an' by: a clean, gray day. 'Every man for hisself,' says Cap'n Sammy, as we drawed near, 'an' the devil take the hindmost. She's a likely-lookin' craft. Pinched fast, too. An' the weather-glass kickin' at its foundations! Eh, Tumm? Every man for hisself.' It turned out Cap'n Sammy was right. She was a tramp, the *Claymore,* two thousand tons, outbound from Liverpool t' Canadian ports, loaded deep, an' now tight in the grip o' the ice. In a big blow o' wind her iron sides would yield like paper t' the crush o' the pack. An' if the signs read true that blow was brewin' in the nor'west. 'Twas breezin' up, down there, with the sky in a saucy temper.

From the deck o' the *Claymore* I looked t' the west, where the little puffs o' wind was jumpin' from, an' t' the sour sky, an' roundabout upon the ice; an' I was glad I wasn't shipped aboard that thin-skinned British tramp, but was mate of a swilin'-steamer, Newf'un'land built, with sixteen-inch oak sides, an' thrice braced with oak in the bows. She was spick an' span, that big black tramp, fore an' aft, aloft an' below; but in a drive o' ice—with the wind whippin' it up, an' the night dark, an' the pack a livin', roarin' whirlpool o' pans an' bergs—white decks an' polished brass don't count for much. 'Tis a stout oak bottom, then, that makes for peace o' mind.

"Cap'n Wrath, at your service, sir: a close-whiskered, bristly, pot-bellied little Britisher in brass buttons an' blue. 'Glad t' know you, Cap'n Small,' says he. 'You've come in the nick o' time, sir. How near can you steam with that ol' batterin'-ram o' yours?'

"'That ol' *what?*" says Cap'n Sammy.

"'Here, some o' you!' Cap'n Wrath yelled t' the crew; 'get a line——'

"'Hol' on!' says Cap'n Sammy; 'no hurry.'

"Cap'n Wrath jumped.

"'Got yourself in a nice mess, isn't you?' says Cap'n Sammy. 'An' in these busy times, too, for us poor swilers. Lost your propeller, isn't you?'

"'No, sir.'

"'Ah-ha!' says Cap'n Sammy. 'Got a weak

blade, eh? Got a crack somewheres in the works, I'll be bound! An' you dassen't use your propeller in this here slob-ice, eh? Scared o' your for'ard plates, too, isn't you? An' you wants a tow, doesn't you? You wants me t' take chances with my blades, eh, an' bruise my poor ol' bows, buckin' this here ice, t' perk your big yelpin' ship t' open water afore the gale nips you?'

"Cap'n Wrath cocked his red head.

" 'Well,' says Cap'n Sammy, 'know what *I* wants? I wants a dram o' rum.'

"Cap'n Wrath laughed. 'Haw, haw, haw!' says he. An' he jerked a thumb for the ship's boy. Seemed t' think Cap'n Sammy was a ol' wag.

" 'We better have that rum in your pretty little cabin,' says Cap'n Sammy, 'an' have it quick, for the weather don't favor delay. I'll want more, an' you'll need more, afore we strikes our bargain. Anyhow, I'm a wonderful hand with a bottle,' says he, 'when it ain't my bottle.'

" 'Haw, haw! Very good, indeed, sir!' says Cap'n Wrath. 'I missed your wink, sir.'

"They went off then, arm in arm, like ol' cronies. 'A dram o' rum, in a little mess like this, sir,' says Cap'n Sammy, 'has heartened many a man afore you.'

"When they come down from the upper deck," Tumm resumed, "Cap'n Sammy was a bit weak in the knees. Tipsy, sir. Ay—Small Sam Small with three sheets in the wind. Free rum an' a fair prospect o' gluttin' his greed had overcome un for once in a way. But grim, sir—an' with little patches o' red aflare in his dry white cheeks. An' as for Cap'n Wrath, that poor brass-buttoned Britisher was sputterin' rage like a Gatlin' gun.

" 'A small difference of opinion, Tumm,' says Cap'n Sammy, 'over North Atlantic towage rates. Nothin' more.'

" 'Get off my ship, sir!' says Cap'n Wrath.

" 'Cap'n Wrath,' says Cap'n Sammy, 'you better take a thoughtful squint at your weather-glass.'

"Cap'n Wrath snarled.

" 'You'll crumple up, an' you'll sink like scrap-iron,' says Cap'n Sammy, 'when that black wind comes down. Take the word for it,' says he, 'of a old skipper that knows the ice from boyhood.'

"Cap'n Wrath turned his back. Never a word from the ol' cock, ecod!—but a speakin' sight of his blue back.

" 'If you works a cracked propeller in this here heavy slob,' says Cap'n Sammy, 'you'll lose it. An' now,' says he, 'havin' warned you fair, my conscience is at ease.'

" 'Off my ship, sir!' says Cap'n Wrath.

" ' 'Twill cost you jus' a dollar a minute, Cap'n Wrath,' says Cap'n Sammy, 'for delay.'

"Cap'n Wrath swung round, with that, an' fair spat rage an' misery in Cap'n Sammy's face.

" 'I'll work the *Bloodhound* near,' says Cap'n

Sammy, 'an' stand by t' take a line. This gale will break afore noon. But give her some leeway, t' make sure. Ay; the ice will feel the wind afore dark. The ice will talk: it won't need no word o' mine. You'll want that line aboard my ship, Cap'n Wrath, when the ice begins t' press. An' I'll stand by, like a Christian skipper, at a dollar a minute for delay'—he hauled out his timepiece—'t' save your ribs from crackin' when they hurts you. Yelp for help when you wants to. Good-day, sir.' He went overside. 'Item, Cap'n Wrath,' says Skipper Sammy, squintin' up: 'to one dollar a minute for awaitin' skipper's convenience.'

"We got under way over the ice, then, for the *Royal Bloodhound*. 'Skipper Sammy,' says I, by an' by, 'was you reasonable with un?'

" 'When I gets what I'm bound t' have, Tumm,' says he, 'they won't be much juice left in that lemon.'

" 'You been lappin' rum, Skipper Sammy,' says I, 'an' you mark me, your judgment is at fault.'

"A squall o' wind near foundered the ol' feller; but he took a reef in his coon-skin coat an' weathered it. 'I'm jus' standin' by the teachin' o' my youth,' says he; 'an' they isn't no meanness in my heart. Give me your hand, Tumm, an' we'll do better in these rough places. How she blows! An' they's a chill comin' down with the wind. My bones is old, Tumm; they hurts me, an' it seems t' me I hears un creak. Somehow or other,' says he, 'I'm all tired out.'

"When we got aboard the *Royal Bloodhound*, Cap'n Sammy bucked the ship within thirty fathoms of the tramp an' lay to. 'Nothin' t' do now, Tumm,' says he, 'but take it easy. All my swilin' life,' says he, 'I been wantin' t' cotch a tramp Britisher in a mess like this; an' now that I *is* cotched one, on my last cruise, I 'low I might as well enjoy myself. I'm all in a shiver, an' I'm goin' t' have a glass o' rum.' An' off he went to his cabin; an' there, ecod! he kep' his ol' bones till long after noon, while the gale made up its mind t' come down an' work its will. Some time afore dark, I found un there still, with a bottle beside un. He was keepin' a little green eye on a Yankee alarm-clock. 'There's another minute gone,' says he, 'an' that's another dollar. How's the wind? Comin' down at last? Good—that's good! 'Twon't be long afore that tramp begins t' yelp. Jus' about time for *me* t' have a dram o' rum, if I'm t' keep on ridin' easy. Whew!' says he, when the dram was down, 'there's three more minutes gone, an' that's three more dollars. Been waitin' all my swilin' life t' squeeze a tramp; an' now I'm havin' a right good time doin' of it. I got a expensive son t' fetch up,' says he, 'an' I needs all the money I can lay my hooks on. There's another minute gone.' He was half-seas-over now: not foundered —he'd ever a cautious hand with a bottle—but well smothered. An' I've wondered since—ay, an' many's the time—jus' what happened up Aloft t' ease off Sam Small's meanness in that hour. He'd never been mastered afore by rum: that I'll be bound for—an' never his own rum. 'I got a expensive son t' raise,' says he, 'an' I wants t' lay my paws on cash. There's another minute gone!' Queer work, this, o' the A'mighty's: rum had loosed the ol' man's greed beyond caution; an' there sot he, in liquor, dreamin' dreams, to his death, for the son of the flaxen girl he'd wronged.

"I stepped outside; but a squall o' soggy wind slapped me in the face—a gust that tweaked my whiskers—an' I jumped back in a hurry t' Skipper Sammy's cabin. 'Cap'n Sammy, sir,' says I, 'the gale's down.'

"'The wind,' says he, 'has the habit o' blowin' in March weather.'

"'I don't like it, sir,' says I.

"'Well,' says he, 'I got a young spendthrift t' fetch up, isn't I?'

"'Still an' all, sir,' says I, 'I don't like it.'

"'Damme, Tumm!' says he, 'isn't you got nothin' better t' do than stand there carpin' at God A'mighty's wind?'

"'They's a big field o' ice t' win'ward, sir,' says I. ''Tis comin' down with the gale; 'twill ram this pack within the hour.'

"'You stand by,' says he, 't' take a line from that tramp when she yelps.'

"Cap'n Sammy, sir,' says I, 'the ship lies badly. She'll never weather——"

" 'Mr. Tumm,' says he, 'you got your orders, isn't you?'

"When Cap'n Sammy fixed his little green squint on me in jus' that frosty way I knowed my duty. 'I is, sir,' says I.

" 'Then,' says he, 'h'ist your canvas. There's another minute gone!'

"By this time the wind was leapin' out o' the nor'west. Fog was come down with the gale, too. 'Twas fallin' thick weather. Comin' on dusk, now, too. The big, black tramp, showin' hazy lights, was changed to a shadow in the mist. The pack had begun t' heave an' grind. I could feel the big pans get restless. They was shiftin' for ease. I could hear un crack. I could hear un crunch. Not much noise yet, though: not much wind yet. But 'twas no fair prospect for the night. Open water—in a shift o' the ice—was but half a league t' the nor'west, a bee-line into the gale's eye. The wind had packed the slob about the ships. It had jammed half a league o' ice against the body o' the big pack t' the sou'east. In the nor'west, too, was another floe. 'Twas there, in the mist, an' 'twas comin' down with the wind. It cotched the first of the gale; 'twas free t' move, too. 'Twould overhaul us soon enough. Ever see the ice rafter, sir? No? Well, 'tis no swift collison. 'Tis horrible an' slow. No shock at all: jus' slow pressure. The big pans rear. They break—an' tumble back. Fields—acres big—slip one atop o' the other. Hummocks are crunched t' slush. The big bergs topple over. It always makes me think o' hell, somehow—the wind, the night, the big white movin' shapes, the crash an' thunder of it, the ghostly screeches. An' the *Claymore's* iron plates was doomed; an' the *Royal Bloodhound* could escape on'y by good luck or the immediate attention o' the good God A'mighty.

"Jus' afore dark I come t' my senses.

"'What's *this!*' thinks I.

"I waited.

"'Wind's haulin' round a bit,' thinks I.

"I waited a spell longer t' make sure.

"'Jumpin' round t' the s'uth'ard,' thinks I, 'by Heavens!' I made for the skipper's cabin with the news. 'Cap'n Sammy, sir,' says I, 'the wind's haulin' round t' the s'uth'ard.'

"'*Wind's what!*' Cap'n Sammy yelled.

"'Goin' round t' the s'uth'ard on the jump,' says I.

"Cap'n Sammy bounced out on deck an' turned his gray ol' face t' the gale. An' 'twas true: the wind was swingin' round the compass; every squall that blew was a point off. An' Cap'n Sammy seed in a flash that they wasn't no dollar a minute for he if Cap'n Wrath knowed what the change o' wind meant. For look you, sir! when the wind was from the nor'west, it jammed the slob against the pack behind us, an' fetched down the floe t' win'ard; but blowin' strong from southerly parts, 'twould not only halt the floe, but 'twould loosen the pack in which we lay, an' scatter it in the open water half a league t' the nor'west. In an hour—if the wind went swingin' round—the *Royal Bloodhound* an' the *Claymore* would be floatin' free. An' round she went, on the jump; an' she blowed high—an' higher yet—with every squall.

"I jumped when I cotched sight o' Cap'n Sammy's face. 'Twas ghastly—an' all in a sour pucker o' wrinkles. Seemed, too, that his voice had got lost in his throat. 'Tumm,' says he, 'fetch my coon-skin coat. I'm goin' aboard Cap'n Wrath,' says he, 't' reason.'

"'You'll never do *that!*' says I.

"'I wants my tow,' says he; 'an' Cap'n Wrath is a warm-water sailor, an' won't know what this ice will do.'

"'Skipper Sammy,' says I, ''tis no fit time for any man t' be on the ice. The pack's goin' abroad in this wind.'

"'I'm used t' the ice from my youth up,' says he, 'an' I'll manage the passage.'

"'Man,' says I, 'the night's near down!'

"'Mr. Tumm, I'm a kindly skipper,' says he, 'but I haves my way. My coon-skin coat, sir!'

"I fetched it.

"'Take the ship, Mr. Tumm,' says he; 'an' stand aside, sir, an you please!'

"Touched with rum, half mad o' balked greed, with a face like wrinkled foolscap, Small Sam Small went over the side, in his coonskin coat. The foggy night fell down. The lights o' the *Claymore* showed dim in the drivin' mist. The wind had its way. An' it blowed the slob off t' sea like feathers. What a wonder o' power is the wind! An' the sea begun t' hiss an' swell where the ice had been. From the fog come the clang o' the *Claymore's* telegraph, the chug-chug of her engines, an' a long howl o' delight as she gathered way. 'Twas no time at all, it seemed t' me, afore we lost her lights in the mist. An' in that black night—with the wind t' smother his cries—we couldn't find Sammy Small.

"The wind fell away at dawn," Tumm went on. "A gray day: the sea a cold gray—the sky a drear color. We found Skipper Sammy, close t' noon, with fog closin' down, an' a drip o' rain fallin'. He was squatted on a pan o' ice—broodin'—wrapped up in his coonskin coat. 'Tumm,' says he, 'carry my ol' bones aboard.' An' he said never a word more until we had un stretched out in his bunk an' the chill eased off. 'Tumm,' says he, 'I got everything fixed in writin', in St. John's, for—my son. I've made you executor, Tumm, for I knows you haves a kindly feelin' for the lad, an' an inklin', maybe, o' the kind o' man I wished I was. A fair lad: a fine, brave lad, with a free hand. I'm glad he knows how t' spend. I made my fortune, Tumm, as I made it; an' I'm glad—I'm proud—I'm mighty proud—that my son will spend it like a gentleman. I loves un. An' you, Tumm, will teach un wisdom an' kindness, accordin' t' your lights. That's all, Tumm: I've no more t' say.' Pretty soon, though, he run on: 'I been a mean man. But I'm not overly sorry now: for hunger an' hardship will never teach my son evil things o' the world God made. I 'low, anyhow,' says he, 'that God is even with me. But I don't know—I don't know.' You see," Tumm reflected, " 'tis wisdom t' *get* an' t' *have*, no doubt; but 'tis not the whole o' wisdom, an' 'tis a mean poor strand o' Truth t' hang the weight of a life to. Maybe, then," he continued, "Small Sam Small fell asleep. I don't know. He was quite still. I waited with un till twilight. 'Twas gray weather still—an' comin' on a black night. The ship pitched like a gull in the spent swell o' the gale. Rain fell, I mind. Maybe, then, Skipper Sammy didn't quite know what he was sayin'. Maybe not. I don't know. 'Tumm,' says he, 'is you marked his eyes? Blood back o' them eyes, sir—blood an' a sense o' riches. His strut, Tumm!' says he. 'Is you marked the strut? A little game-cock, Tumm—a gentleman's son, every pound an' inch of un! A fine, fair lad. My lad, sir. An' he's a free an' genial spender, God bless un!'

"Skipper Sammy," Tumm concluded, "died that night."

"We found Skipper Sammy squatted on a pan of ice."

The gale was still blowing in Right-an'-Tight Cove of the Labrador, where the schooner *Quick as Wink* lay at anchor: a black gale of fall weather.

"Tumm," the skipper of the *Quick as Wink* demanded, "what become o' that lad?"

"Everybody knows," Tumm answered.

"What!" the skipper ejaculated; "you're never tellin' me he's the Honor——"

"I is," Tumm snapped, impatiently. "He's the Honorable Samuel Small, o' St. John's. 'If I'm goin' t' use my father's fortune,' says he, 'I'll wear his name.' "

" 'Twas harsh," the skipper observed, "on the mother."

"No-o-o," Tumm drawled; "not harsh. She never bore no grudge against Small Sam Small—not after the baby was born. She was jus' a common ordinary woman."

IX

AN IDYL OF RICKITY TICKLE

IX

AN IDYL OF RICKITY TICKLE

NO fish at Whispering Islands: never a quintal—never so much as a fin—at Come-by-Chance; and no more than a catch of tom-cod in the hopeful places past Skeleton Point of Three Lost Souls. The schooner *Quick as Wink*, trading the Newfoundland outports in summer weather, fluttered from cove to bight and tickle of the coast below Mother Burke, in a great pother of anxiety, and chased the rumor of a catch around the Cape Norman light to Pinch-a-Penny Beach. There was no fish in those places; and the *Quick as Wink*, with Tumm, the clerk, in a temper with the vagaries of the Lord, as manifest in fish and weather, spread her wings for flight to the Labrador. From Bay o' Love to Baby Cove, the hook-and-line men, lying off the Harborless Shore, had done well enough with the fish for folk of their ill condition, and were well enough disposed toward trading; whereupon Tumm resumed once more his genial patronage of the Lord God A'mighty, swearing, in vast satisfaction with the trade of those parts, that all was right with the world, whatever might seem at times. "In this here world, as Davy Junk used t' hold," he laughed, in extenuation of his improved philosophy, " 'tis mostly a matter o' fish." And it came about in this way that when we dropped anchor at Dirty-Face Bight of the Labrador, whence Davy Junk, years ago, in the days of his youth, had issued to sail the larger seas, the clerk was reminded of much that he might otherwise have forgotten. This was of a starlit time: it was blowing softly from southerly parts, I recall; and the water lay flat under the stars—flat and black in the lee of those great hills—and the night was clear and warm and the lights were out ashore.

"I come near not bein' very *fond* o' Davy Junk, o' Dirty-Face Bight," Tumm presently declared.

"Good Lord!" the skipper taunted. "A rascal you couldn't excuse, Tumm?"

"I'd no fancy for his *religion,*" Tumm complained.

"What religion?"

"Well," the clerk replied, in a scowling drawl, "Skipper Davy always 'lowed that in this here damned ol' world a man had t' bite or get bit. An' as for his manner o' courtin' a maid in consequence——"

"Crack on!" said the skipper.

And Tumm yarned to his theme. . . .

"Skipper Davy was well-favored enough, in point o' looks, for fishin' the Labrador," he began; "an'

I 'low, with the favor he had, such as 'twas, he might have done as well with the maids as the fish, courtin' as he cotched—ay, an' made his everlastin' fortune in love, I'll be bound, an' kep' it at compound interest through the eternal years—had his heart been as tender as his fear o' the world was large, or had he give way, by times, t' the kindness o' soul he was born with. A scrawny, pinch-lipped, mottled little runt of a Labrador skipper, his face all screwed up with peerin' for trouble in the mists beyond the waters o' the time: he was born here at Dirty-Face Bight, but sailed the *Word o' the Lord* out o' Rickity Tickle, in the days of his pride, when I was a lad o' the place; an' he cotched his load, down north, lean seasons or plenty, in a way t' make the graybeards an' boasters blink in every tickle o' the Shore. A fish-killer o' parts he was: no great spectacle on the roads o' harbor, though—a mild, backward, white-livered little man ashore, yieldin' the path t' every dog o' Rickity Tickle. 'I gets my fish in season,' says he, 'an' I got a right t' mind my business between whiles.' But once fair out t' sea, with fish t' be got, an' the season dirty, the devil hisself would drive a schooner no harder than Davy Junk—not even an the Ol' Rascal was trappin' young souls in lean times, with revivals comin' on like fall gales. Neither looks nor liver could keep Davy in harbor in a gale o' wind, with a trap-berth t' be snatched an' a schooner in the offing; nor did looks hamper un in courtship, an' that's my yarn, however it turns out, for his woe or salvation. 'Twas sheer perversity o' religion that kep' his life anchored in Bachelors' Harbor—'A man's got t' bite or get bit!'

"Whatever an' all, by some mischance Davy Junk was fitted out with red hair, a bony face, lean, gray lips, an' sharp an' shifty little eyes. He'd a sly way, too, o' smoothin' his restless lips, an' a mean habit o' lookin' askance an' talkin' in whispers. But 'twas his eyes that startled a stranger. Ah-ha, they was queer little eyes, sot deep in a cramped face, an' close as evil company, each peekin' out in distrust o' the world; as though, ecod, the world was waitin' for nothin' so blithely as t' strike Davy Junk in a mean advantage! Eyes of a wolf-pup. 'Twas stand off a pace, with Davy, on first meetin', an' eye a man 'til he'd found what he wanted t' know; an' 'twas sure with the look of a Northern pup o' wolf's breedin', no less, that he'd search out a stranger's intention—ready t' run in an' bite, or t' dodge the toe of a boot, as might chance t' seem best. 'Twas a thing a man marked first of all; an' he'd marvel so hard for a bit, t' make head an' tale o' the glance he got, that he'd hear never a word o' what Davy Junk said. An' without knowin' why, he'd be ashamed of hisself for a cruel man. 'God's sake, Skipper Davy!' thinks he; 'you needn't be afeared o' *me! I* isn't goin' t' touch you!' An' afore he knowed it he'd have had quite a spurt o' conversation with Davy, without sayin' a word, but merely by means o' the eyes; the upshot bein' this: that he'd promise not t' hurt Davy, an' Davy'd promise not t' hurt he.

"Thereafter—the thing bein' settled once an' for all—'twas plain sailin' along o' Davy Junk.

" 'Skipper Davy,' says I, 'what you afeared of?'

"He jumped. 'Me?' says he, after a bit. 'Why?'

" 'Oh,' says I, 'I'm jus' curious t' know.'

" 'I've noticed, Tumm,' says he, 'that you is a wonderful hand t' pry into the hearts o' folk. But I 'low you doesn't mean no harm. That's jus' Nature havin' her way. An' though I isn't very fond o' Nature, I got t' stand by her dealin's here below. So I'll answer you fair. Why, lad,' says he, '*I* isn't afeared o' nothin'!'

" 'You're wary as a wolf, man!'

" 'I bet you I *is!*' says he, in a flash, with his teeth shut. 'A man's *got* t' be wary.'

" 'They isn't nobody wants t' hurt a mild man like you.'

" 'Pack o' wolves in this here world,' says he. 'No mercy nowhere. You bites or gets bit.'

"Well, well! 'Twas news t' the lad that was I. 'Who tol' you so?' says I.

" 'Damme!' says he, 'I found it out.'

" 'How?'

" 'Jus' by livin' along t' be thirty-odd years,'

" 'Why, Skipper Davy,' says I, 'it looks t' me like a kind an' lovely world!'

"'You jus' wait 'til you're thirty-two, like me,' says he, 'an' see how you likes it.'

"'You can't scare *me,* Skipper Davy!'

"'World's full o' wolves, I tells you!'

"'Sure,' says I, 'you doesn't *like* t' think that, does you?'

"'It don't matter what I likes t' think,' says he. 'I've gathered wisdom. I thinks as I must.'

"'I wouldn't believe it, ecod,' says I, 'an I knowed it t' be true!'

"An' I never did."

Tumm chuckled softly in the dark—glancing now at the friendly stars, for such reassurance, perhaps, as he needed, and had had all his genial life.

"A coward or not, as you likes it, an' make up your own minds," Tumm went on; "but 'twas never the sea that scared un. 'They isn't no wind can scare me,' says he, 'for I isn't bad friends with death.' Nor was he! A beat into the gray wind—hangin' on off a lee shore—a hard chance with the Labrador reefs in foggy weather—a drive through the ice after dark: Davy Junk, clever an' harsh at sea, was the skipper for *that,* mild as he might seem ashore. 'Latch-string out for Death, any time he chances my way, at sea,' says he; 'but I isn't goin' t' die o' want ashore.' So he'd a bad name for drivin' a craft beyond her strength; an' 'twas none but stout hearts—blithe young devils, the most, with a wish t' try their spirit—would ship on the *Word o' the*

Lord. 'Don't you blame *me* an we're cast away,' says Davy, in fair warnin'. 'An you got hearts in your bellies, you keep out o' *this.* This here coast,' says he, 'isn't got no mercy on a man that can't get his fish. *An' I isn't that breed o' man!*' An' so from season t' season he'd growed well-t'-do: a drive in the teeth o' hell, in season—if hell's made o' wind an' sea, as I'm inclined t' think—an' the ease of a bachelor man, between whiles, in his cottage at Rickity Tickle, where he lived all alone like a spick-an'-span spinster. 'Twas not o' the sea he was scared. 'Twas o' want in an unkind world; an' t'was jus' that an' no more that drove un t' hard sailin' an' contempt o' death—sheer fear o' want in the wolf's world that he'd made this world out t' be in his own soul.

" 'Twas not the sea: 'twas his own kind he feared an' kep' clear of—men, maids, an' children. Friends? Nar a one—an' 'twas wholly his choosin', too; for the world never fails t' give friends t' the man that seeks un. 'I doesn't *want* no friends,' says he. 'New friends, new worries; an' the more o' one, the more o' the other. I got troubles enough in this here damned world without takin' aboard the thousand troubles o' friends. An' I 'low they got troubles enough without sharin' the burden o' mine. *Me* a friend! I'd only fetch sorrow t' the folk that loved me. An' so I don't want t' have nothin' t' do with nobody. I wants t' cotch my fish in season—an' then I wants t' be left alone. Hate or love: 'tis all the same—trouble for the hearts o' folk on both sides. An', anyhow, I isn't got nothin' t' do with this world. *I'm* only lookin' on. No favors took,' says he, 'an' none granted.' An', well—t' be sure—in the way the world has—the world o' Rickity Tickle an' the Labrador let un choose his own path. But it done Davy Junk no good that any man could see; for by fits he'd be bitter as salt, an' by starts he'd be full o' whimpers an' sighs as a gale's full o' wind, an' between his fits an' his starts 'twas small rest that he had, I'm thinkin'. He'd no part with joy, for he hated laughter, an' none with rest, for he couldn't abide ease o' mind; an' as for sorrow, 'twas fair more than he could bear t' look upon an' live, for his conscience was alive an' loud in his heart, an' what with his religion he lived in despite of its teachin'.

"I've considered an' thought sometimes, overcome a bit by the spectacle o' grief, an' no stars showin', that had Davy Junk not been wonderful tender o' heart he'd have nursed no spite against God's world; an' whatever an' all, had he but had the power an' wisdom, t' strangle his conscience in its youth he'd have gained peace in his own path, as many a man afore un.

"'Isn't *my* fault!' says he, one night. 'Can't blame *me!*'

"'What's that, Skipper Davy?'

"'They says Janet Luff's wee baby has come t' the pass o' starvation.'

"'Well,' says I, 'what's *your* tears for?'

"'I isn't got nothin' t' do with this here damned ol' world,' says he. '*I'm* only lookin' on. Isn't no good in it, anyhow.'

"'Cheer up!' says I. 'Isn't nobody hurtin' *you.*'

"'Not bein' in love with tears an' hunger,' says he, 'I isn't able t' cheer up.'

"'There's more'n that in the world.'

"'Ay; death an' sin.'

"I was a lad in love. 'Kisses!' says I.

"'A pother o' blood an' trouble,' says he. 'Death in every mouthful a man takes.'

"'Skipper Davy,' says I, 'you've come to a dreadful pass.'

"'Ay, an' t' be sure!' says he. 'I've gathered wisdom with my years; an' every man o' years an' wisdom has come to a dreadful pass. Wait 'til you're thirty-two, lad, an' you'll find it out, an' remember Davy Junk in kindness, once you feels the fangs o' the world at your throat. Maybe you thinks, Tumm, that I likes t' live in a wolf's world. But I doesn't like it. I jus' knows 'tis a wolf's world and goes cautious accordin'. I didn't make it, an' don't like it, but I'm here, an' I'm a wolf like the rest. A wolf's world! Ah-ha! You bites or gets bit down here. Teeth for you an you've no teeth o' your own. Janet Luff's baby, says you? But a dollar a tooth; an'—I *keeps* my teeth; keeps un sharp an' ready for them that might want t' bite me in my old age. If I was a fish I'd be fond o' angle-worms; bein' born in a wolf's world, with the soul of a wolf, why, damme, I files my teeth! Still an' all, lad, I'm a genial man, an' I'll not deny that I'm unhappy. You thinks I likes t' hear the lads ashore mock me for a pinch-penny an' mean man? No, sir! It grieves me. I wants all the time t' hear the little fellers sing out: "Ahoy, there, Skipper Davy, ol' cock! What fair wind blowed *you* through the tickle?" An' I'm a man o' compassion, too. Why, Tumm, you'll never believe it, I knows, but *I* wants t' lift the fallen, an *I* wants t' feed the hungry, an' *I* wants to clothe the naked! It fair breaks my heart t' hear a child cry. I lies awake o' nights t' brood upon the sorrows o' the world. That's my heart, Tumm, as God knows it—but 'tis not the wisdom I've gathered. An' age an' wisdom teach a man t' be wary in a wolf's world. 'Tis a shame, by God!' poor Davy Junk broke out; 'but 'tisn't *my* fault!'

"I was scared t' my marrow-bones.

" 'An' now, Tumm,' says he, 'what 'll I do?'

" 'Skipper Davy,' says I, 'go wash the windows o' your soul!'

"He jumped. 'How's that?' says he.

" ' 'Twould ease your heart t' do a good deed,' says I. 'Go save that baby.'

" 'Me!' says he, in a rage. 'I'll have no hand whatever in savin' that child.'

" 'Why not?'

" ' 'Twouldn't be kind t' the child.'

" 'God's sake!'

" 'Don't you *see,* Tumm?'

" 'Look you, Skipper Davy!' says I, 'Janet's baby isn't goin' t' die o' starvation in *this* harbor. There'll be a crew o' good women an' Labrador hands at Janet's when the news get abroad. But an you're lucky an' makes haste you'll be able t' get there first.'

" 'What's *one* good deed?'

" " 'Twould *be* a good deed, Skipper Davy,' says I. 'An' you'd *know* it.'

"Skipper Davy jumped up. An' he was fair shakin' from head t' toe—with some queer temptation t' be kind, it seemed to me then.

" 'Make haste!' says I.

" 'I can't do a good deed!" he whimpered. 'I—I—got the other habit!'

" 'Twas of a June night at Rickity Tickle that Davy Junk said these words," Tumm commented, in a kindly way, "with the Labrador vessels fitted out an' waitin' for a fair wind: such a night as this—a slow, soft little wind, a still, black harbor, an' a million stars a-twinkle." He paused—and looked up from the shadowy deck of the *Quick as Wink.* "What more can a man ask t' stay his soul," he demanded, "than all them little stars?" The skipper of the *Quick as Wink* said, " 'Tis a night o' fair promise!" And Tumm, in a sigh, "Davy Junk would never look up at the stars." And the little stars themselves continued to wink away in companionable reassurance just the same.

"The other habit!" Tumm ejaculated. "Ay—the other habit! 'Twas habit: a habit o' soul. An' then I learned a truth o' life. 'Twas no new thing, t' be sure: every growed man knows it well enough. But 'twas new t' me—as truth forever comes new t' the young. Lovely or fearsome as may chance t' be its guise, 'tis yet all new to a lad—a flash o' light upon the big mystery in which a lad's soul dwells eager for light. An' I was scared; an' I jumped away from Davy Junk—as once thereafter I did—an' fair shook in the Presence o' the Truth he'd taught me. For 'twas clear as a star: that a soul fashions its own world an' lives therein. An' I'd never knowed it afore! An' I mind well that it come like a vision: the glimpse of a path, got from a hill—a path the feet o' men may tread t' hell an men perversely choose it. A wolf's world? A world as you likes it! An' in my young world was no sorrow at all—nor any sin, nor hate, nor hunger, nor tears. But love, ecod!—which, like truth, comes new t' the young, an' first glimpsed is forever glorious. I was sixteen then—a bit more, perhaps; an' I was fond o' laughter an' hope. An' Bessie Tot was in my world: a black-haired, red-lipped little rogue, with gray eyes, slow glances, an' black lashes t' veil her heart from eager looks. First love for T. Tumm, I'm bold t' say; for I'm proud o' the odd lift o' soul it give me—which I've never knowed since, though I've sought it with diligence—ay, almost with prayer. I've no shame at all t' tell o' the touch of a warm, moist little hand on the road t' Gull Island Cove—the whisper, the tender fear, in the shadow o' the Needle—an' the queer, quick little kiss at the gate o' dark nights—an' the sigh an' the plea t' come again. An' so, t' be sure, I'd no kin with the gloom o' Davy Junk that night, but was brother t' hope an' joy an' love. An' my body was big an' warm an' willin'—an' my heart was tender—an' my soul was clean—an' for love o' the maid I loved I'd turned my eyes t' the sunlit hills o' life. God's world o' sea an' labor an' hearts—an' therein a lad in love!

"'I'll take care o' my soul,' thinks the lad, that was I, 'lest it be cast away forever, God help me!'

"An' that's youth—the same everywhere an' forever."

Tumm sighed. . . .

"'Twas high time for me now t' sail the Labrador," Tumm resumed, "an' I was in a pother o' longin' t' go. Sixteen—an' never a sight o' Mugford! I was fair ashamed t' look Bessie Tot in the eye. Dear heart!—she ever loved courage in a man, an' the will t' labor, too, an' t' be. An' so—'Ecod!' thinks I, on the way home that night, 'I'll sail along o' Davy Junk, an' prove my spirit, withal, for the whole world t' see. An' I 'low that *now*, knowin' me so well as he does, Davy'll ship me.' But my mother said me nay—until I pestered her skirts an' her poor heart beyond bearin'; an' then all at once she cried, an' kissed me, an' cried a bit more, an' kissed me again, an' hugged me, an' 'lowed that a lad had t' be a man *some* time, whatever happened, an' bade me sail along o' Skipper Davy an he'd take me, which he never would do, thinks she. It come about, whatever an' all, that I found Skipper Davy on the doorstep of his spick-an'-span cottage by Blow-Me, near the close o' that day, with night fallin' with poor promise, an' the wind adverse an' soggy with fog. An' thinks I, his humor would be bad, an' he'd be cursin' the world an' the weather an' all, in the way he'd the bad habit o' doin'. But no such thing; he was as near to a smile o' satisfaction with hisself as Davy Junk could very well come with the bad habit o' lips an' brows he'd contracted. For look you!—a scowl is a twist o' face with some men; but with Davy his smile was a twist that had t' be *kep'* twisted.

" 'Evil weather, Skipper Davy,' says I.

" 'Oh no,' says he. 'It all depends on how you *looks* at it.'

" 'But you're not in the habit o' lookin'——'

" 'I'm learnin' t' peep,' says he.

"I'd no means of accountin' for *that!* 'Foul weather, an' no talkin', man,' says I, 'for the Labrador bound!'

"'What's the sense o' naggin' the *weather?*' says he. 'Isn't you able t' leave her alone, Tumm? Give her time, lad, an' she'll blow fair. She've her humors as well as we, haven't she? An' she've her business, too. An' how can *you* tell whether her business is good or evil? I tells you, Tumm, you isn't got no right t' question the weather.'

"'God's sake!' says I. 'What's happened overnight?'

"'No matter,' says he. 'I 'low a man haves the right t' *try* a change o' mind an he wants to.'

"'Parson Tree been overhaulin' you?'

"'Oh,' says he, 'a man can put his soul shipshape without the aid of a parson.'

"'Then, Skipper Davy,' says I, with my heart in my mouth, 'I 'low I'll sail the Labrador along o' you.'

"'Not so, my son,' says he. 'By no means.'

"'I *wants* to, Skipper Davy!'

"'You got a mother ashore,' says he.

"'Well, but,' says I, 'my mother says a lad's got t' be a man *some* time.'

"'I can't afford t' take you, Tumm.'

"'Look you, Skipper Davy!' says I, 'I'm able-bodied for my years. None more so. Take me along o' you—an' I'll work my hands t' bloody pulp!'

"''Tis not that, Tumm,' says he. ''Tis—well—because—I've growed kind o' fond o' you overnight. We got a bit—intimate—together—an' you—was kind. 'Tis not my habit, lad, t' be fond o' nobody,' says he, in a flash, 'an' I'll not keep it up. I'm otherwise schooled. But, damme!' says he, 'a man's got t' go overboard *once* in a while, whatever comes t' pass.'

"'Then sure you'll take me!'

"'I wouldn't get my fish,' says he. 'I'd be scared o' losin' you. I'd sail the *Word o' the Lord* like a ninny. Thinks I—I got t' be careful! Thinks I—why, I can't have Tumm cast away, for what would his mother do? Thinks I—I'll reef, an' I'll harbor, an' I can't get along, an' I might hit ice, an' I might go ashore on Devil-May-Care. *An' I wouldn't get my fish!*'

"'Still an' all, I *got* t' go!'

"'You isn't driven,' says he.

"'Skipper Davy,' says I, fair desperate, 'I got a maid.'

"'A *what?*' says he.

"'A maid, Skipper Davy,' says I, 'an' I wants with all my heart t' prove my courage.'

"'What you goin' t' do with her?'

"'I'll wed her in due season.'

"Skipper Davy jumped—an' stared at me until I fair blushed. I'd shook un well, it seemed, without knowin'—fair t' the core of his heart, as it turned out—an' I'd somehow give un a glimpse of his own young days, which he'd forgot all about an' buried in the years since then, an' couldn't now believe had been true. 'A maid?' says he then. 'A—

maid! An' you'll wed her in due season! *You,* lad! Knee-high to a locust! An' you wants t' go down the Labrador t' prove your courage for the sake of a maid? For—Love! 'Tis not a share o' the catch you wants—'tis not altogether the sight o' strange places—'tis not t' master the tricks o' sailin' —'tis not t' learn the reefs an' berths o' the Labrador. 'Tis t' prove—your—courage! An' for the sake of a maid! Is that the behavior o' lads in the world in these times? Was it always the way—with lads? I wonder—I wonder an *I* might ever have done *that*—in my youth!'

"I couldn't tell un.

" 'Tumm,' says he, 'I'll further your purpose, God help me!'

"An' then the first adventure comin' down like a patch o' sunshine over the sea! Ah-ha, the glory o' that time! Sixteen—an' as yet no adventure beyond the waters of our parts! A nobbly time off Mad Mull in a easterly wind—a night on the ice in the spring o' the year—a wrecked punt in the tickle waters; but no big adventure—no right t' swagger—none t' cock my cap—an' no great tale o' the north coast t' tell the little lads o' Rickity Tickle on the hills of a Sunday afternoon. But now, at last, I'd a berth with Davy Junk, a thing beyond belief, an' I was bound out when the weather fell fair. An' out we put, in the *Word o' the Lord,* in good time; an' Skipper Davy—moved by fear of his fondness, no doubt—cuffed me from Rickity Tickle t' the Straits, an' kicked me from the Barnyards t' Thumb-an'-Finger o' Pinch-Me Head. 'I isn't able t' be partial, lad,' says he, 't' them I'm fool enough t' be fond of.' Whatever had come to un overnight at Rickity Tickle—an' however he'd learned t' peep in new ways—there was no sign o' conversion on the cruise from Rickity t' Pinch-Me. But 'twas some comfort t' be well in the lead o' the fleet in the Straits, when a westerly gale blowed the ice off-shore, an' it fair healed my bruises an' cured my dumps t' get the traps down between the Thumb an' the Finger afore a sail showed up in the gray weather t' s'uth'ard. Hard sailin', every inch o' the way down—blind an' mad. Skipper Davy at the wheel: fog alongshore, ice in the fog, reefs off the heads, an' a wind, by times, t' make the *Word o' the Lord* howl with the labor o' drivin' north.

"I didn't ease up on my prayers afore the anchor was down an' the *Word o' the Lord* got her rest in the lee o' Pinch-Me.

" 'Feelin' better, Tumm?' says Skipper Davy.

" 'I is.'

" 'Don't you mind them few little kicks an' cuffs,' says he; 'they was jus' meant t' harden you up.'

" 'My duty,' says I.

" 'I isn't very used t' bein' fond o' nobody,' says he, 'an' 'tis on my conscience t' make a man o' your mother's son. An', moreover,' says he, ' 'tis on my conscience t' teach you the worth of a dollar in labor.'

" 'My duty, Skipper Davy.'

" 'Oh,' says he, 'you don't owe me nothin', I'm deep in debt t' you.'

" 'Twas a harsh season for Labrador-men. Fish? Fish enough—but bitter t' take from the seas off Pinch-Me. The wind was easterly, raw, wet, an' foggy, blowin' high an' low, an' the ice went scrapin' down the coast, an' the big black-an'-white seas come tumblin' in from Greenland. There was no lee for the *Word o' the Lord* in that weather: she lied off the big cliffs o' Pinch-Me, kickin' her heels, writhin' about, tossin' her head; an' many's the time, in the drivin' gales o' that season, I made sure she'd pile up on the rocks, in the frothy little cove between the Thumb an' the Finger, where the big waves went t' smash with a boom-bang-swish an' hiss o' drippin' thunder. By day 'twas haul the traps—pull an oar an' fork the catch with a back on fire, cracked hands, salt-water sores t' the elbow, soggy clothes, an' an empty belly; an' by night 'twas split the fish—slash an' gut an' stow away, in the torch-light, with sticky eyelids, hands an' feet o' lead, an' a neck as limp as death. I learned a deal about life—an' about the worth of a dollar in labor. 'Take that!' says Skipper Davy, with the toe of his boot, 'an' I'm sorry t' have to do it, but you can't fall asleep on a stack o' green cod at two o'clock in the mornin' an' be a success in life. Try *that!*'

says he, with the flat of his hand, 'though it grieves me sore t' hurt you.' But whatever an' all, us loaded the *Word o' the Lord*—an' stowed the gear away, an' fell down t' sleep in our tracks, an' by an' by lied in wait for a fair wind t' the Newf'un'land outports. An' there comes a night—a fine, clear, starry night like this—with good prospects o' haulin' out at break o' day. An' I could sleep no longer, an' I went on deck alone, t' look up at the sky, an' t' dream dreams, maybe, accordin' t' my youth an' hope an' the good years I'd lived at Rickity Tickle.

"A lovely night: still an' starlit—with a flash o' northern lights abroad, an' the ol' *Word o' the Lord* lyin' snug asleep in a slow, black sea.

"Skipper Davy come up. 'Tumm,' says he, 'is you on deck?'

" 'Ay, sir.'

" 'Where is you, b'y?'

" 'Lyin' here, sir,' says I, 'cuddled down on a cod-net.'

" 'Now that the labor is over,' says he, 'I'm all tired out an' downcast.' He sot down beside me. 'You doesn't bear no malice for all them kicks an' cuffs, does you?' says he. 'You sees, lad, I—I—isn't used t' bein' fond o' nobody—an' I 'low I don't know how very well—though I done my best.'

" 'Sure,' says I, 'I've no malice?'

" 'What you doin' here?' says he.

" 'Lookin' up at the stars.'

" 'Is you?' says he. 'What for?'

" 'They're such wonderful friendly little beggars, Skipper Davy!'

" '*I* never looks up at the stars.'

" 'They're friends o' *mine!*'

" 'Not bein' very much in favor o' the world!' says he, 'I doesn't countenance the stars.'

"An' all at once I turned to un in a sweat an' shiver o' fear. Not countenance the stars! Here, then, another flash o' light upon the big mystery! Now first I glimpsed the end of a path of evil. Not countenance the stars! Could a man truly come t' such a sad pass in God's good world? I knowed evil: all lads knows it, t' be sure—its first gates in the world: not its last places. An' they stand without, in fair meadows, an' peep beyond—an' wonder, an' ponder, an' wish with all their young, eager hearts t' follow the paths an' learn. An' we that are growed forget the wonder an' the wish—an' show no scars that we can hide, an' draw the curtain upon our ways, an' make mockery o' truth, an' clothe our hearts in hypocrisy, an' offer false example, an' lie of our lives an' souls, lest we stand ashamed. 'Tis a cruel fate for lads, it may be, an' a deceitful prophecy. I knows little enough about life, but exhibit my ways, whatever an' all, for the worth they may have; an had I my will in the world, I'd light the country beyond the gates, ecod! an' with my own hands stir up all the beasts! Not countenance the stars! 'Twas a vision again for the lad that was I—first glimpse o' the end of any path of evil. 'I must guard my soul,' thinks the lad that was I, in his heart, 'lest I come to a pass like this.'

"There was light abroad by this time: a big, golden, jolly moon, peepin' over the black cliffs o' Thumb-an'-Finger, not ashamed t' grin its fellowship with sea an' stars an' all the handiwork o' God. An' all the world save Davy Junk—all the world from the ragged hills t' the rim o' the sea—from the southern stars fair north t' the long, white lights—was at peace in the night. An' then Skipper Davy said: 'I done jus' what you tol' me, Tumm, afore us put out from Rickity Tickle. I—I—done a deal for Janet Luff's child—an' I've no complaint t' make. I made haste, lad, as you said, an' got there first, an' done the good deed, an' knowed 'twas a good deed; an' I been a sight happier ever since—though I'm woebegone enough, God knows! But the windows o' my soul is cleaner. I'm awakened. I been sort o' converted—t' love. An' comin' down the coast—an' here at the fishin', with the gales ill-minded an' steeped in hate, an' the Thumb an' the Finger jus' waitin' t' le'ward t' pinch us all t' death—I been broodin' a deal upon love. An' I'm lonely. An' now, Tumm, I wants t' get married—as a lonely man will. An' they's a maid back there at Rickity Tickle that I loved in my youth. She've a kind heart and a comely face. She was ever kind—an' comely. I told her once, long ago, at Dirty-Face Bight, that I—I—sort o' fancied I loved her; an' I 'lowed that once I found out that I did in truth—an' once I'd laid up a store against evil times—that I—I—I'd ask her t' wed me. An' I knowed that I loved her all the time. An' she said—that she'd wait. An' she've—waited. I 'low, Tumm, that you might help me in this pass—for you're young, an' in love, an' in touch with the ways o' courtship, an' I'm old, an' crabbed, an' tired, an' afraid o' the world, an' I've no admiration for the man that I is. Eh, Tumm, lad? Think you might—serve me?'

"'Skipper Davy,' says I, 'I'll do my level best.'

"'A fair night,' says he. 'Breezin' up a bit from the north. I 'low we'll get underway at dawn. Is you—is you—well acquainted with Mary Land?'

"'Sure,' says I, 'she nursed me!'

"'She's the maid,' says he, 'that's waited.'

"'An' you,' says I, in a rage, 'is the man she've waited for all these years?'

"'I 'low,' says he, 'you might move her t' heed me.'

"'Well,' says I, 'I'll do what I'm able—for she.'

"'I'm much obliged,' says he; 'an' I forgives you all the grief them cuffs an' kicks has caused me.'

"An' so it come t' pass that when the *Word o' the Lord* dropped anchor in Rickity Tickle—an' when I was foot-loose from the ol' craft an' had kissed my mother t' the dear woman's satisfaction—

an' Bessie Tot on the sly as near t' my own as I could manage—an' when I'd swaggered the roads a bit—an' had cocked my cap, as I'd planned t' do, an' made mention o' Mugford an' Pinch-Me an' easterly weather—I spread my sails on the road t' Gull Island Cove t' warn Mary Land o' the queer news I had. She'd a place in my heart, an' in the hearts of us all, for her goodness an' wise ways—a large, warm place in mine, like a sister's nook in a young lad's heart. An' sure she was sister t' all the lads o' Rickity Tickle—love in her touch, wisdom on her lips, an' faith in her eyes. A Newf'un'land maid: buxom now, an' still rosy an' fair an' blue-eyed an' tender. But not merry at all: gone too far in years, I used t' think, for folly t' flush an' dimple her—she was goin' on thirty—but as it was, as then I knowed, too much grieved for waste o' merriment. An' when she'd hugged me, her nurseling, as she used t' say—an' when she'd noted my stride an' the spread o' my feet—an' had marked my elderly talk an' praised my growth—I told her my errand. I plumped it out, without mercy, in the way of a lad; an' she took it ill, I thought; for breath left her, an' she stared like death. An' then she begun t' cry—an' then she sobbed that she was wonderful happy—an' then she dried her poor eyes—an' then she named Davy Junk an' the good God in one long breath o' love an' thanks—an' then she smiled. An' after that she put her warm arms around me an' half hid her sweet motherly face; but yet I could see that she was flushed an' dimpled, like any young maid o' the place, an' that her eyes were both merry an' wet. An' I marveled t' learn that youth an' joy would come back in a flash o' time as soon as love beckoned a finger.

"'I loves un, Toby!' says she. 'I jus' can't help it.'

"'He've poor timber in his soul,' says I.

"She'd have none o' that! 'Oh no,' says she; 'he jus' needs—me.'

"'A poor stick for looks,' says I.

"'Ah, but,' says she, 'you didn't know un when he was *young,* Toby.'

"'Pst!' says I. 'An' he've kep' you waitin' a long time.'

"'It haven't been hard t' wait,' says she; 'for I jus' *knowed* he'd come—when ready.'

"'I'll fetch Skipper Davy this night.'

"'Ay,' says she. 'I'm—wonderful happy.'

"'There'll be guns goin' at a weddin' in Rickity Tickle afore long,' says I, 'I'll be bound!'

"She laughed like a maid o' sixteen. 'An', ecod!' says she, 'I got a new muslin all ready t' wear!'

"It rained on Rickity Tickle that night: no lusty downpour—a mean, sad drizzle o' cold mist. The road t' Gull Island Cove was dark as death—sodden underfoot an' clammy with wet alder-leaves. Skipper Davy come with fair courage, laggin' a bit by the way, in the way o' lovers, thinks I, at such times.

An' I'd my hand fair on the knob o' Mary Land's door—an' was jus' about t' push in—when Skipper Davy all at once cotched me by the elbow an' pulled me back t' the shadows.

" 'Hist!' says he.

" 'Ay?'

" 'Did you—tell her outright—that I'd *take* her?'

" 'Ay, sure!'

" 'No help for it, Tumm?'

" 'God's sake!' says I.

" 'I—I—I won't!' says he.

"An' he fled—ay, took t' the heels of un, an' went stumblin' over the road t' Rickity Tickle in the dark. I listened—helpless there at Mary Land's door—while he floundered off beyond hearin'. An' 'twas hard—a thing as bitter as perdition—t' tell Mary Land that he'd gone. T' break her heart again! God's sake! But she said: 'Hush, Toby! Don't you mind for me. I—I'm not mindin'—much. I'm used—t' waitin'.' An' then I made off for Davy Junk's spick-an'-span cottage by Blow-Me t' speak the words in my heart. Slippery rock an' splash o' mud underfoot—an' clammy alder-leaves by the wayside—an' the world in a cold drench o' misty rain—an' the night as dark as death—an' rage an' grief beyond measure in my heart. An' at last I come t' Davy Junk's cottage by Blow-Me, an' forthwith pushed in t' the kitchen. An' there sot Davy Junk, snuggled up to his own fire, his face in his hands, woebegone an' hateful of hisself an' all the world—his soul lost, not because he'd failed in love for a maid, or worked woe in a woman's heart, but because in fear o' the world he'd lived all his years in despite o' love, an' love had left un for good an' all, t' make the best of his way alone through the world he feared. He'd not look at me at all, but shifted in his chair, an' rubbed his hands, an' snuggled closer to his own fire, an' whimpered what I couldn't make out. Nor would I speak t' he afore he turned t' face me—though I'd hard labor enough t' keep my words in my throat. Whatever an' all, at last he turned. An' 'twas the old Davy Junk come t' Rickity Tickle again—the beast o' fear peerin' out from his soul through his little, mean eyes. An' I might have loathed un then—had I not pitied un so greatly.

"'I made a mistake, Tumm,' says he.

"'Ay, Skipper Davy.'

"'This here world's a wolf's world,' says he, with his teeth bared. 'An', damme, I got enough t' do t' fend for myself!'

"'Skipper Davy,' says I, 'you go t' hell!'

"'Twas the first oath ever I uttered with intention. An' I ran straightway t' Billy Tot's cottage—t' cure the taste o' the thing on my lips—an' t' ease the grief in my heart—an' t' find some new store o' faith for my soul. An' I kissed Bessie Tot fair on her rosy check in the middle o' the kitchen floor without carin' a jot who seed me."

It was the end of the yarn of Davy Junk, of Dirty-Face Bight; but Skipper Jim, of the *Quick as Wink,* being of a curious turn, presently inquired:

"What become o' Davy?"

"Lost with the *Word o' the Lord,"* Tumm replied, "with all hands aboard."

"Went down in wreck," the skipper observed, "an' left nothin' but a tale."

"A tale with a moral," said I.

"Ay, an' t' be sure!" Skipper Jim agreed. "Davy Junk left a tale—with a moral."

"Damme!" Tumm exploded, " 'tis as much as most men leaves!"

And the little stars winked their own knowledge and perfect understanding of the whole affair.